If she'd stayed still, quiet, then maybe he could have resisted her.

But felt her fingers on his jaw, gently brus g the night's stubble. Then she whi d his name and ripped every last tre of his resolve to tatters. His hands fou r waist and she slid onto his lap. He kis er, heat banking and flaring in his che il his head began to swim.

I st kiss could be explained away as a b the moment thing, the second trashed t cular excuse. They both knew exactly y were doing. Her gaze was locked v and he heard her murmur his name, f ips against his in a smile.

oured everything he had, everything into the kiss, letting the long, slow beat o passion take him.

Dear Reader

When I was planning this book, one of the things I pondered long and hard was where to set it. I wanted somewhere exciting, interesting, possibly a little challenging. Romantic, definitely. And although I've been to many places that would answer that description exactly, none of them quite seemed to fit the bill as the backdrop for this story.

The answer turned out to be in the very last place that I thought of looking: quite literally, right on my doorstep.

Like many big cities, London is a place of shifting populations. People come from all over the world—as tourists, to study, or to work—and Dr Adam Marshall is one of those people. He's in London for a month, and soon he'll be moving on.

Dr Jenna Weston knows just what it's like to be left behind. She's promised herself that she's not going to allow her future to follow the pattern of her past, and that if she opens her heart again it's going to be to someone who'll stay with her. So right from the start Adam's completely wrong for Jenna—despite the fact that his good looks and charm set her pulse racing.

Thank you for sharing Adam and Jenna's story with me. I loved writing it, and I hope you enjoy reading it. I'm always delighted to hear from readers, and you can e-mail me via my website at www.annieclaydon.com

Annie

DOCTOR ON
HER DOORSTEP

BY
ANNIE CLAYDON

All the characters in this book have no existence outside the imagination of the author, and have no relation whatsoever to anyone bearing the same name or names. They are not even distantly inspired by any individual known or unknown to the author, and all the incidents are pure invention.

First published in Great Britain 2012
by Mills & Boon, an imprint of Harlequin (UK) Limited.
Harlequin (UK) Limited, Eton House,
18-24 Paradise Road, Richmond, Surrey TW9 1SR

© Annie Claydon 2012

ISBN: 978 0 263 89167 6

Harlequin (UK) policy is to use papers that are natural, renewable and recyclable products and made from wood grown in sustainable forests. The logging and manufacturing process conform to the legal environmental regulations of the country of origin.

Printed and bound in Spain
by Blackprint CPI, Barcelona

Cursed from an early age with a poor sense of direction and a propensity to read, **Annie Claydon** spent much of her childhood lost in books. After completing her degree in English Literature, she indulged her love of romantic fiction and spent a long, hot summer writing a book of her own. It was duly rejected and life took over, with a series of U-turns leading in the unlikely direction of a career in computing and information technology. The lure of the printed page proved too much to bear, though and she now has the perfect outlet for the stories which have always run through her head, writing Medical™ Romance for Mills and Boon. Living in London, a city where getting lost can be a joy, she has no regrets about having taken her time in working her way back to the place she started from.

Why not check out Annie's fantastic debut?

ALL SHE WANTS FOR CHRISTMAS

**Also available in eBook format
from www.millsandboon.co.uk**

There are so many people to thank.
My family and friends, who believed in me
with such certainty that sometimes I feared for their
sanity. The talented and lovely Medical Romance
writers, who have welcomed this new recruit to
their ranks with such warmth and kindness.
And last (but not least) the editorial team at
Harlequin Mills & Boon, especially Lucy Gilmour, who
has guided me with insight, patience and good humour
every step of the way. My heartfelt thanks to you all.

CHAPTER ONE

JENNA had been longing for this moment. She slid her car into the parking space outside the rambling Victorian house that had once been her family home and killed the ignition. A shower and a pizza were waiting for her inside and nothing now stood between her and the solitary, relaxing evening she had promised herself.

There was something, though. Some*one* to be more precise, and he was sitting on the steps, in the shade of the wide arch of the porch, his elbows propped on his knees, legs stretched out in front of him. His demeanour said he was waiting for someone, and since that someone was unlikely to be her, he must be another of Janice's endless stream of boyfriends.

It was a shame, but she couldn't do anything about it. Janice had moved out of the ground-floor flat three weeks ago, and if she hadn't seen fit to share her forwarding address with him, then Jenna certainly wouldn't. The best she could do for him was to take a contact number and promise to pass it on.

Okay. This won't take long. Pity really. She didn't like giving people the brush-off and there was something about his relaxed pose that said he was someone you'd like to spend time with. Jenna hauled the two heavy shopping bags out of the boot of her car and manoeuvred her way through the front gate, kicking it closed behind her, rather harder than she had meant to. The low sun dazzled her, and she was halfway down the front path before she could get a proper look at the stranger.

He looked like a rock star. Distressed leather jacket, jeans and boots. Light brown hair streaked with gold, which was just long enough to slick behind his ears, and the kind of tan you didn't get from a two-week Easter break. His eyes were hidden behind dark glasses but the tilt of his head indicated that he was watching Jenna as she walked towards him and dumped her shopping bags at his feet.

'Hello. Can I help you?'

'I'm looking for Dr Weston.'

'Oh! That's me.' Something crawled up Jenna's spine, and she wondered whether a bug had got into her shirt. A bug that was somehow making her fingertips tingle as well.

'I'm Adam Sinclair. Dr Greene told me he'd mentioned my name to you.' His accent was English, but he'd obviously been in America for a while. Mid-Atlantic. Rolling between the familiar, cut-glass consonants of home and a heart-stopping drawl.

'He said…' Jenna gulped back the words. It wasn't tactful to repeat what Rob Greene had said in his email. 'I thought you weren't going to arrive until next weekend.' Jenna's reflection stared back at her from the dark lenses of his glasses.

He seemed to realise that the sunglasses were unnerving her and he pulled them off, hooking them into the open neck of his shirt. 'I flew in from America this morning, and I'm driving down to Exeter tonight for the week. I thought I'd swing by and try to see you on the way.'

His tawny gaze looked as if it had been kissed by the

same sun as his hair and was a hundred times more unsettling. Jenna fixed her eyes on a point somewhere between the bridge of his nose and his hairline and issued a mental instruction to pull herself together. 'That's something of a detour. North London's not exactly on the way from Heathrow to the M3.'

'Well, I did say swing. Implies an arc.' He shrugged off the twenty miles of crowded roads as if they were a minor obstacle. 'Is there a problem?'

'No.' Jenna didn't move. It wasn't really a problem. He just wasn't quite what she'd been expecting. To be absolutely honest, she wouldn't have known *how* to expect someone like this, appearing out of nowhere, on her doorstep.

'I should show you some ID.' He'd mistaken her bewilderment for mistrust, and pulling his wallet out of his jacket pocket he opened it and handed it to her. Credit cards. A Florida driving licence. A photograph of a woman. Jenna closed the wallet and handed it back.

'Thanks.' She reached for her bags of shopping, but he got there first, picking them up as he got to his feet. 'You'd better come inside.'

Adam followed her up the stairs to her flat in silence, keeping his distance as she opened her front door and waiting for her to motion him in. He followed her through to the kitchen and put her bags onto the counter.

'I'll just put my shopping away, and then show you the flat.' Jenna threw her keys down on the countertop and slipped out of her jacket, rolling up the cuffs of the plain white shirt she wore underneath. 'Would you like a cup of tea?'

'Tea would be nice, thanks.' He had retreated back to stand in the doorway, obviously intent on not crowding her. 'I'm getting the feeling that I'm not quite what you expected.'

He could say that again. 'Well, actually, I somehow got the idea that you were a woman from Rob's email. But it makes no difference.'

There was a whole world of difference in the wry grin that melted his chiselled good looks. No medical doctor had any business even being in possession of a smile like that, let alone using it.

'Ah. Sorry about that. If you'd prefer not...'

'It's not a problem. Rob does tend to write as if he's being charged by the word.' Rob's characteristically staccato email had, as usual, provided more questions than answers. *Travelling alone, concerns about hotel. Security and quiet needed. Speak on return from hols.* Rob wasn't back for another week and in the meantime Jenna had jumped to the conclusion that Dr Sinclair was a woman.

'Yeah. When Ellie was born he emailed me a photo of her and Cassie, and wrote *"7 lbs. Beautiful"* underneath. I sent him a text demanding details and he replied *"Girl"*.'

Jenna snorted with laughter. 'He sent you a photo? You were honoured, most of us just got *"Born"* with a couple of exclamation marks. You've known Rob a while, then, as Ellie's nearly five.'

'Ever since med school. Ellie was born just after I went abroad.' He gave her a confiding grin and Jenna hung on to the countertop for support. 'If it wasn't for Cassie I'd never know what he was up to, though. She sends photos, letters. Even had a copy made of that drawing they have in their sitting room of Ellie and Daisy.'

He was clearly aware that she was alone in the house, and was trying to drop as many reassuring details into the conversation as he could. By chance, the reference turned out to be particularly appropriate. 'That sketch is one of mine. Cassie asked me to do a second copy for a friend who was overseas.' Someone who was going through a tough time, Cassie had said.

Laughter escaped his studied reserve. 'Really? That drawing is remarkable, I have it hung in my study at home. It always makes me smile.'

It was only a pencil sketch. Jenna had been pleased with how it had turned out, but it was nothing all that special. He seemed to want to say more, but she cut him short before he got the chance. 'I hear Florida's a beautiful part of the world. What do you do there?' Jenna opened the refrigerator and started to stack her shopping away.

'I'm a plastic surgeon.'

So this was the image that sold nose jobs and liposuction to the rich, was it? Adam probably did pretty well out of it. Jenna reckoned that a good percentage of the female population would go through hell, high water and even general anaesthesia to see approval in Adam Sinclair's face.

Taking advantage of the fact that the open fridge door hid her from him, Jenna rolled her eyes. 'And that's what you're going to be lecturing on?'

'Yes. I was looking to spend some time back in the UK and when I got the offer of a month here as a visiting lecturer, I jumped at it. I'm spending a week visiting family, and I'll be back here on Sunday week for my first lecture.'

'On a Sunday? It's a public lecture, then.' Not that she was even vaguely interested.

'Yeah. Three o'clock in the Fleming Lecture Theatre.'

He didn't invite her to come, and Jenna didn't express any interest in doing so. Instead, she straightened up, flashing him a brisk smile. 'I'll make the tea and take you downstairs to see the flat.' Perhaps she'd been too harsh in judging him. Okay, so Adam wasn't a woman.

That was hardly his fault, neither was it a crime, although that smile of his ought to be kept under house arrest. If he chose to use his talents and an expensive education to carry out largely unnecessary surgery, that was a matter for his own conscience. He was what he was.

As a sign of penitence she picked up a packet of chocolate biscuits, along with her mug and the keys to the ground-floor flat, before leading him down the stairs. 'I've just had the walls done, and it stinks of paint at the moment, but it'll air out by next week.'

'That's fine. I just want somewhere to stay. Rob offered to put me up, but with two children and another one on the way he doesn't have the room. And I don't like hotels much.'

'No. Rob mentioned that.' Jenna led the way into the lounge and plumped herself down on the dust sheet that covered the sofa.

'He did?' The look he shot her was half-wary. Three-quarters guilty.

'In passing. I don't much like hotels either.' It wasn't her business. Jenna reached for the biscuits as a change of subject, opening the packet and offering him one. 'Why don't you take a look around? There isn't much furniture, I'm afraid, just the basics.'

'That's what I like about it.' He ignored the biscuits and walked over to the window, drawing the shutters back to let the evening sun spill into the room, slanting across the walls and floor. 'And there's plenty of light.' He turned to Jenna. 'This will be fine, if that's okay with you.'

'Don't you want to look at the rest?'

'Should I?' He gave her a quizzical look, and Jenna felt the back of her neck begin to burn.

'It's the usual practice. I'll stay here if you don't mind.' She felt awkward under his gaze, the way the corners of his mouth twitched slightly when he looked at her spare frame and her dark red hair, scraped back off her face and secured tightly at the back of her head. His profession, and those smouldering tawny eyes, seemed to make a constant, unspoken judgement of her.

'So you're not going to come with me and point out the finer features of the property?'

'No, I take a relaxed approach. Drink tea and let you show yourself around.'

He chuckled. 'Fine. I can take a hint.' He disappeared out into the hallway, the sound of his footsteps indicating his progress around the flat. He was back again almost before she could extract a second biscuit from the packet. 'One of the doors is locked.'

'Ah, yes. That's the second bedroom. My last tenant went to Spain to work and she's left some of her stuff here for me to send on when she gets settled. I can clear the boxes out if you want that room, but the main bedroom's through here.' Jenna led him the full length of the hallway and opened the door.

He strode inside and looked around. 'Big room.' He sat down on the bed. 'Decent mattress. That's a real bonus.'

'I think you'll find that's my line. As I'm here, I'll also point out that there's plenty of cupboard space.'

'Which would be my cue to look inside.'

'Absolutely. Let me know if you find any skeletons. I don't think Janice left any behind, but you never can be sure.'

Adam opened the doors wide, inspecting the interior of the wardrobe. The smile that was playing around his lips broadened when Jenna jumped as he flinched back suddenly. 'Nope. She must have taken them all with her.'

'Well, that's a relief.' Jenna brushed a few crumbs from the front of her shirt. 'What do you think, then?'

His eyes travelled around the bedroom. 'May I see the other room, please? The one that's locked.'

'Of course.' Jenna led the way down the hallway. 'This room's a little smaller and there isn't so much cupboard space. I like it better, though, there are doors out on to the patio and you get the early morning sun.' Most tenants preferred the extra cupboard space.

The soft leather of his jacket brushed against her arm as he walked past her into the room. 'I like it too. Would it be okay if I swapped the boxes over to the main bedroom and brought the bed through here?'

Jenna shrugged. 'I'll do that some time next week for you.'

He shook his head. 'No. I'll do it.' He didn't wait for her answer and turned to walk over to the French doors, staring out into the garden. 'Big garden. What's the area at the end there that's attracting the butterflies?'

Her beloved butterfly garden. Jenna was both pleased and slightly embarrassed that he'd noticed it. 'That's part of the garden too. My grandfather and I planted it when I was little. There are herbs and shrubs to attract the butterflies, but it's getting a bit out of control now.'

'So this was your family home?'

'Yes. It was my grandparents' house. I split it into two flats after they died. I was a student then and the income came in handy.' He nodded as if he understood, but there was no way that he could have done. Jenna herself didn't fully understand what had happened with her parents.

'You lived with your grandparents?'

'Yes, I've lived here since I was ten.'

He said nothing. Jenna began to wish that either she'd not said so much or that he would question her more. Anything but this half-story, which he seemed to accept so unquestioningly. Or maybe it wasn't acceptance. Maybe he simply didn't care.

Adam turned away from the window and followed her through to the sitting room. 'So, do we get to haggle over the rent now?'

She'd rather he didn't. That way he had of quirking his eyebrow gave him an unfair advantage. 'It's seven hundred for the month. I'll stock the fridge up for you.'

'You will not. Seven hundred pounds is daylight robbery, this place is worth twice that. I may have been away for a while, but I haven't lost touch with London property prices.'

'I keep the rent low so I can pick and choose who I have here. Anyway, you can't haggle upwards.'

'Why not?' He lifted one eyebrow.

'You just can't. I won't have it.'

He held up his hands in a gesture of surrender. 'Okay. Done.' Adam reached into his jacket and brought out his wallet. 'Would you like a deposit?'

'Not particularly. The place is empty anyway.'

'Fair enough.' He picked his mug of tea up from the coffee table and took a final swig. 'I'd better get back on the road, then, and leave you to get on with your supper.'

Jenna flushed. He'd noticed that she was already on her third chocolate biscuit and was regarding the packet pointedly. So what? She was on her feet all day in a busy A and E department, not sitting in a leather chair behind a swanky desk, and she worked up an appetite. And she might not have curves, but at least her figure owed nothing to silicone. 'Thanks. I'll see you in a week's time, then.'

CHAPTER TWO

SUNDAY morning. Ten-thirty. Jenna should have been drinking tea and reading the paper, but instead she was studying the street outside. A car drew up and she twitched the muslin curtains back into place, stepping away from the big bay windows.

The bell sounded when she was halfway down the stairs. As soon as she opened the door, a four-year-old bundle of energy launched itself at her.

'Hello, Ellie. Did you have a nice holiday?' She nodded at Rob and crooked her finger at him. 'Come in. You've got some explaining to do.'

Nothing was going to dent Rob's good humour this morning or dim the violent hue of his Cornwall Surfers T-shirt. He followed Jenna up the stairs, replying indulgently to Ellie's chatter, and flung himself into an armchair while Jenna fetched some juice, a pad of paper and a box of assorted pencils and crayons for Ellie.

'Don't give her that pad, Jen. She'll only make a mess of it.' Rob was looking at the thick, white cartridge paper that Jenna had put in front of Ellie.

Jenna nodded at Ellie, who was smoothing her hand across the pad. 'You're never too young to be able to appreciate the texture of nice paper.' She bent and tore one of the thick sheets from the pad, clipping it on to a board for Ellie, and selected a soft pencil from the box. 'Here you are, sweetie, try using this.'

Rob rolled his eyes. 'Well, if she turns out to be the next Picasso, then I suppose we'll have you to thank. Look, sorry about the mix-up last week.'

'We managed.' Jenna walked through to the kitchen to make some tea and Rob followed her. 'You might have told me, though.'

'Well, it's a bit tricksy, you know how these things are.'

'No, not really, not until you tell me.'

'Okay, well, Adam's a decent bloke. One of the best people I've ever known, in fact, but he's not had it easy these last eighteen months. I've been trying to find him somewhere to stay where he can have some peace and quiet, get back on his feet.' Rob shrugged. 'Tactfully, you know?'

Rob was no good at tact, he usually left that kind of thing to Cassie. 'Which explains all that cloak-and-dagger stuff in your email.'

'Yeah.' Rob brightened. 'Yeah, that's it.' It wasn't it at all. There was a whole list of other questions that sprang to mind.

'So he's not staying with you and Cass?'

'No. We offered, of course, but he says that we've no room. And what with Cass being pregnant and everything...' They both jumped as the doorbell went. If that was Adam, he was early.

'Can you get the intercom?' Jenna reached up into the kitchen cabinet for another cup. 'And don't worry. He'll be fine here, and I'll keep an eye on him.'

'Thanks, Jen.'

Rob disappeared out of the kitchen and Jenna gave the teapot a swirl, even though she'd already done so once, and dumped it down on the tray. It would have helped if she knew what on earth she was meant to be keeping an eye out for, but Cassie would be a much better bet than Rob when it came to straight answers.

The commotion in the hallway indicated that the object of her speculation had arrived and that he was being greeted by both Ellie and her father at the same time, the child squealing with laughter and demanding a hug.

Jenna popped her head around the kitchen doorway. He was a picture of health and good humour, tanned, taller and broader than Rob and grinning as he lifted Ellie up so she could fling her arms around his neck. No trace of whatever it was that Rob was so concerned about.

'Hello, there.' His head jerked upwards as Jenna spoke.

'Hi.' He came forward, still carrying Ellie, who looked as if she was going to have to be prised away from him with a crowbar. 'I hope we're not crashing in on your morning.'

'Not at all. Welcome back.' She held her hand out to him, and he took it, his touch cool, measured. He seemed to be less careful about keeping his distance now that he was not alone with her, and held on to her hand for one moment too long before Jenna pulled hers back again.

'Where *is* my present?' Ellie was demanding now, beating her hands against his shoulders.

'In a minute, honey. We'll just collect the keys from Jenna and get out of her hair first.' He was smooth, she'd give him that. Perfect poise. Nothing but easy charm.

'I've just made tea.' Jenna waved him into the sitting room. 'And Ellie's been doing some drawing, I expect you'll be wanting to see that. Let her open her present here if she'd like to.'

When she brought the tea in, Ellie was already working on the package that Adam had given her. Pink paper on the outside, a pretty bow and layer upon layer of paper underneath, firmly bound with sticky tape.

'Hope it lives up to all this anticipation.' Rob was making no move to help his daughter as she whooped with delighted frustration, trying to rip the parcel open.

'Me, too.' Adam too was letting Ellie get on with the task of unwrapping her present unaided. 'So how was the holiday? Catch any waves?'

'Fabulous. We were on the north coast, and the hotel was close to this great little surf beach, so I could go out first thing in the morning and make it back in time for breakfast.'

'Nice one. You'll have to come back to Florida soon.' Adam accepted a mug of tea from Jenna, taking a grateful sip.

'We will. You can sit on the beach with Cassie and the kids and I'll show you how it's done.'

'Yeah, right, in your dreams.' He shot a bright grin at Jenna. 'Takes more than a hideous T-shirt to make a surfer. What was Cassie thinking, letting you go out in that?'

Rob laughed. 'She reckons that if I go out in it then she won't have to put up with it around the house.' He ran his hand over the garishly coloured fabric. 'What, don't you like it?'

Ellie's delighted squeal meant that Adam never did get to deliver his verdict. She'd reached the inside of the package and was holding up a string of beads.

'Aren't they pretty?' Ellie brought the beads to Jenna to show her and when she examined them carefully she could see they were hand painted, each one different.

'I got them in Mexico.' Adam watched as Jenna carefully wound the beads around Ellie's neck for her, nodding with approval. 'You look beautiful, honey.'

Ellie was climbing up on the sofa, between Adam and

Rob, to catch a glimpse of herself in the mirror over the fireplace, and Rob tugged at her sleeve. 'What else have you got, then, El?' He gestured to the folded fabric that still lay amongst the ruins of the wrapping paper.

Ellie pulled the fabric out, turned it around a couple of times then held it up against herself, and Jenna caught a glimpse of colourful embroidery on a white cotton background.

'It's a bit big, isn't it, mate?' Rob was surveying his daughter. 'She'll be sixteen before she grows into that.'

'No, idiot. It's a dress.' Jenna smoothed the fabric and held it against Ellie. It was roomy, but the drawstring at the waist meant that it could be adjusted to fit her perfectly.

'Can I wear it?' Ellie was jumping up and down with excitement.

'Not until you've said the magic word.' Rob smiled at her.

Ellie launched herself at Adam, nearly knocking his tea over and flung her arms around his neck, kissing his cheek. 'Oh, that's nice... Can I have another one? Right here?' His finger was on his other cheek and Ellie obliged eagerly. 'Thank you.'

'I drew you a picture.' Ellie's hands were on Adam's shoulder, pulling as hard as she could, and Jenna saw alarm flare in Rob's face.

'Gently, El. Adam's shoulder isn't properly mended yet.'

Adam waved him away. 'I'd love to see your picture, Ellie, will you show me?'

Ellie fetched her drawing and climbed up onto Adam's knee. 'That's Mum...and Dad...me and Daisy...and that's you.' Her finger was moving across the paper.

'That's very good. And who's this, up there?'

Ellie shook her head, as if the stupidity of adults never ceased to amaze her. 'That's your friend. Mum says she's in heaven.'

Rob's face tightened, but Adam's smile never faltered. 'That's lovely, honey. I'm so pleased you drew her too, along with the rest of us.'

'Will you tell her?'

'Ellie…' There was a note of anxiety in Rob's voice but Adam's glance quieted him.

'Of course I'll tell her. She'll be so happy, I expect she'll tell all her friends up there.'

Ellie glared up at the ceiling and nodded, as if satisfied. 'Can I wear my dress?'

This time Adam allowed Rob to step in. 'Not yet, El. We've got some things to move around downstairs and I don't want you getting it all dirty. Later on, when we've finished.'

The circular face that Ellie had drawn, giving no hint of who Adam's friend might really be, released its grip on Jenna's attention and she bumped back down to earth. 'Oh, no, that's okay, I already did that.'

Adam's gaze was on her now, so palpable that it almost tickled her skin. 'You did what?'

'I moved the boxes and the bed. And put a few things in the fridge, just essentials, to keep you going until to-morrow.'

His eyes slid down her thin bare arms, and her fingers jerked in her lap. 'On your own? I thought I said I'd do that.'

Rob came to her rescue. Kind of. 'What I love about this woman is that you can say anything you like to her, and she'll hear you, but she won't listen. Eh, Jen?'

Adam pursed his lips thoughtfully. 'In that case, perhaps I can just put my bag downstairs and take you all to lunch before my lecture.' He glanced at Ellie, his face breaking into a smile. 'Go and ask your dad if you can wear your new dress.'

The dress fitted perfectly. Adam and Rob had disappeared downstairs with the keys, while Jenna stripped off Ellie's jeans and T-shirt and drew the dress over her head, running her fingers over the hand embroidery and arranging it just so.

'Can I have some perfume?' Ellie was obviously keen on playing the lady.

'No, you know what your mum says about perfume.' Ellie's idea of a dab behind her ears was to tip half a bottle of Cassie's anniversary gift over her head. 'Tell you what, this is much better.'

She trimmed a couple of stalks of lavender from the bunch in the fireplace and tied them firmly with a ribbon from the drawer. 'Here, I'll fix it onto your dress… like this…and you'll smell nice and look nice as well.' She leaned back and admired her handiwork. Ellie looked beautiful.

'Are you going to dress up, too?' Ellie had unpinned Jenna's hair and was arranging it around her shoulders.

'No, I'm fine as I am.' Jenna looked down at her jeans and cotton, sleeveless top. This was about as good as it got, and however much she wanted to make an effort to look nice today she wasn't going to do anything that might betray that to either Rob or Adam.

'Perfect.' Adam's voice boomed behind her and she jumped. He obviously meant Ellie.

'Doesn't she look pretty?' She flashed a smile at him.

'Yes, she looks perfect, too.' His mouth twisted in a smile as Jenna flushed. 'Thank you for the flowers.'

She'd arranged lavender and sweet-smelling greenery in a vase, putting it downstairs in the hearth to break up the stark, white walls and bring a little of the garden into the flat. And he'd noticed them. 'They're not really flowers.'

He shrugged. 'Thanks anyway. You have a good eye, they look stunning.' He ignored the redness, which was now spreading across her cheeks, and turned his attention to Ellie. 'And you look like a proper young lady.'

Ellie seemed to take as much delight as Jenna did in Adam's approval, but she was more straightforward about showing it. 'I did Jenna's hair, too. Look.' She tugged at one of Jenna's curls.

'Maybe I'll just fix it back up again.' Jenna gathered her hair behind her head, looking for the elastic tie that Ellie had discarded somewhere on the floor. She'd never quite got around to liking her hair much. Too many memories of her mother tugging mercilessly at the tangles and bemoaning the fact that it wasn't smooth like her sister's. And that, horror of horrors, it was red.

'Don't.' Something about Adam's tone made her freeze, stock still. 'It really suits you like that.' There was no indication in his face that this was anything other than a polite compliment.

Rob came to her rescue again. Friendly, open and perfectly unmoved by the intensity of Adam's voice. 'Yeah. Fiery, eh, Jen? Doesn't take any nonsense from anyone.' He gave Adam a pointed look and held his hand out to Ellie. 'Come on, then. If we're going, let's go.'

'Flame-haired.' Rob missed Adam's quiet comment in the kerfuffle of getting Ellie out of the door and down the stairs, but Jenna caught it, as she guessed she had been meant to. She shot him a glare and he grinned innocently, as if he'd meant nothing by it. Maybe he hadn't.

'So what's the story with Julie, then?' Adam had waited until Rob had taken Ellie home and he and Jenna were sitting alone in the open-air enclosure on the pavement outside the restaurant.

'Julie? You mean Julie Taylor?'

'Yes. Her consultant, Iain Simms, emailed me on Friday evening, copying you in.'

'Oh. I haven't had time to look at my email for the last couple of days.' He was making her feel self-conscious again. His eyes had wandered towards her far too many times already, cool, assessing, as if he was sizing her up, and Jenna couldn't help wondering what he saw. Wishing that it wasn't what she saw in the mirror. Pale limbs, untouched by the sun. A slim waist, but precious few curves. Red hair.

If he noticed her agitation, he paid no heed to it, leaning forward across the table towards her. 'Too busy dragging furniture and boxes around, eh?'

Actually, yes. Those golden eyes were far too perceptive for Jenna's liking. And she didn't want him to see the effect they had on her when she met his gaze. 'Shall we walk?' Walking seemed a better option than sitting here, staring straight at him.

'If you like.' He stretched his arms, flexing his shoulder as if it was stiff, and signalled for the bill. 'Along the river? Somehow the river always makes me feel as if I'm home again.'

Jenna nodded. The pavement to one side of them dipped and meandered its way down to the south bank of the Thames. Tower Bridge was in the distance to the right. The footbridge to their left, with a stream of Sunday afternoon day-trippers dawdling their way across the river. 'I've never been away long enough to have that feeling of coming home. I'd like to travel. Learn a little about life.'

'You don't need a plane ticket to learn about life.' His eyes focussed somewhere else for a moment, as if he was straining to catch a last glimpse of the place he had left behind. 'Let's walk. I'll tell you what Iain's email said.'

They strolled together down the broad steps that led to the river path. He was all sun-drenched charm, relaxed grace, and Jenna allowed herself to wonder what it would be like to walk arm in arm with him. She gave herself twenty seconds to feel the warmth of his body next to hers and then consigned the fantasy to the breeze that blew in from the river.

'So I guess we'll be working together on this one.'

'Uh?' If she'd been listening then she would know what they were working together on. 'You mean you're going to be working at the hospital? As well as lecturing?'

The slight twitch of his eyebrow told her that he'd already said that. 'Yeah. Iain's asked me to work with him on a few specific cases. I'm also working down in A and E for one or two days a week, while Dr Bryant's on paternity leave. I'm hoping to get the chance to observe some of the techniques and practices you employ.'

'And teach us a thing or two as well?' The idea of being observed for any length of time by those amber eyes was... well, it would be interesting, if nothing else.

'Yes. That too. I do have something to offer in return.'

'I'm sure you do.' Jenna wasn't even going to think about what Adam had to offer. 'So why your particular interest in Julie? We're hoping that she won't need much reconstructive surgery.'

'It's not all about surgery.' He grinned down at Jenna. 'Iain suggested that since you've been visiting her every day, I should speak to you about her.'

'Well, I only really know about her case in a general sense. I saw Julie when she came into A and E after she was the victim of an acid attack. She saw it coming and shielded her face, but she has burns on her arm and shoulder. Iain and his team are dealing with that, though I'm really more concerned about her emotional state.'

'Which is where I come in.'

Jenna turned to him in surprise. There was nothing in his face, no clue of what he was thinking. As she stared, a small muscle at the side of his jaw broke free of his control and began to flicker. 'You know something about trauma?'

He knew something all right. That muscle was going crazy. 'I do. Many of my patients are in the same position as Julie, and I try to deal with that as well as their physical needs.'

Jenna narrowed her eyes. 'And there's no counselling help? In Florida?'

He seemed to relax a little. 'I work for a charity. We work all over South America, bringing medical aid and surgery to poor communities. Florida's our home base. We have a facility there where patients who need specialised care are brought.'

'So...' Embarrassment trickled down the back of her neck and made her shiver. She'd misjudged Adam.

'So what?' It appeared he wasn't going to let her off the hook.

'I thought...' She heaved a sigh. She might as well spit it out. 'When you said plastic surgery and Florida, I thought you meant nip and tuck.'

'Ah.' Amusement sounded in his voice. 'No, I mostly deal with cleft lips, cleft palates, facial tumours, injuries. Mostly children and teenagers, some adults. I imagine the rich and famous expect their surgeons to turn up to work in something other than ripped jeans and a T-shirt.'

Jenna swallowed hard. He would be eye-catching enough in pretty much anything, and she didn't want to even think about ripped jeans. His neat chinos and plain, casual shirt were quite enough for the time being. 'Then I owe you an apology. Your work sounds amazing.'

'It has its rewards.' The warmth in his face told Jenna that those rewards weren't measured in pounds and pence. 'Many of my patients are traumatised, either from their injuries or from having been mocked or shunned because of their appearance. I told Iain that I was especially interested in seeing how that was dealt with here.'

Jenna shrugged. 'That's just the trouble. Julie won't see a counsellor.'

'So I hear. I also hear that she trusts you and that you've been doing your best to fulfil that role for her.' He fixed her with an enquiring look. 'Not a particularly easy path to tread. Difficult not to become over-involved, I imagine.'

Jenna pressed her lips together and he shrugged as if he had already proved his point. 'My lecture starts in an hour. Would you like to come?'

'I might just do that. Were you thinking of covering trauma?'

'I was considering touching on the fact that a small team with limited resources needs to take a more holistic approach.'

'In other words you need to treat the person, not just the injury.' It was a private dream of Jenna's. Not just to be a doctor but to be a healer. 'Difficult not to become over-involved, then.'

A smile spread slowly across his face. 'I'm going to have to take the Fifth on that.'

'If you do that, the jury's going to assume that the answer's yes.'

'Nothing I can do about that. They can assume whatever they like.' For a moment Jenna thought that she had broken through his reserve. Then the fire died in his eyes. 'I'll drop in and see Julie tomorrow.'

Jenna nodded. He wasn't making a request and she supposed that she was going to be stuck with his input, whatever that might be. She may as well accept it gracefully. 'I'd be interested to hear what you think. You know where to find me.'

'I do.' He looked at his watch. 'It's time I headed over to the lecture theatre. Will you fill me in on some more of Julie's details on the way?'

It was the dream that had haunted him for the last eighteen months, sometimes once every week or two, sometimes every night. He woke up with a stifled cry, icy sweat against his cheek. For a moment, he couldn't work out where he was, and then the dim glow of the nightlight brought him to his senses. The muslin drapes, drawn across the half-open French doors, fluttered in the night breeze and he slowly got out of bed, shaking his head, trying to reclaim his place in the waking world.

Slipping outside onto the moss-lined stones of the patio, he took a deep draught of air, inhaling the smell of the city, mingling with the softer scents of the garden. He started, instinctively drawing back into the shadows, as a sharp click sounded above his head.

Jenna had opened the door, which led on to an iron railed balcony above his head, and was standing beside the steps that snaked down to the patio, just a few feet away from where he stood. In the darkness Adam could see only that she wore something loose, swirling around her bare feet, and that her hair was a wild shadow around her head.

He held his breath. She was leaning over the balcony, craning round towards him, and he guessed that she could see the open French doors and the light inside. Adam flattened himself against the wall and watched as she seemed to sniff the air, like some shy, nocturnal creature of the forest.

A fox trotted across the lawn. Her head jerked upwards and she followed its progress, waiting until it had disappeared into the shrubbery before she turned and slowly walked back into the house. Adam heard the catch on the door being fastened and then there was silence.

He swiped his hand across his face. Tomorrow was going to be a busy day, and he should try to sleep again. The thought that she was there, perhaps even watching over him, calmed him. Tomorrow would be time enough to probe the intriguing contradictions of his flame-haired, disturbingly gorgeous landlady.

CHAPTER THREE

'LOOK, she's here now.' Julie's face lit up into a grin and Adam turned to see Jenna entering the ward. Red hair, bound tightly at the back of her head, white shirt and dark slacks. Even in such severe attire she looked like an angel. Not one of those sweet, dimpled ones, looking down dispassionately from the safety of a cloud. She was a warrior angel, the kind you'd really like to have on your side when things got tough, who rushed in where everyone else feared to tread and plucked you out of danger.

'She comes every lunchtime, does she?' Adam knew that she did. Iain had already told him that.

'Yes. Just for half an hour. Sometimes less.' There was a hint of resentment in Julie's voice and Adam reflected just how precious that time was for Jenna. A snatched half-hour when most of the A and E staff were happy just to grab a sandwich and get their breath for a few minutes.

Before he had time to answer, Jenna was at the foot of the bed, her fingers grasping the rail where Julie's notes hung. 'Hi, there.' She was all smiles. 'How are you, then? You're looking better.'

Julie flashed her a grin. 'Yeah, I feel better. That other doctor says I'm doing okay. They've got the pain control sorted now.'

'Good.' Jenna's gaze caught Adam's and he basked in

its warmth for a moment before her attention was back on Julie. 'I see you've met Dr Sinclair.'

'Yes.' Julie turned her wide blue eyes on to Adam. 'He's going to monitor my progress.'

Jenna's face lit up. She looked a great deal more enthusiastic about it than she had the other day but, then, she'd obviously enjoyed his lecture, questioning him about it all the way home. 'Really? That's good. You've made plenty already.'

'Suppose so.' A porter wheeled a squeaking trolley into the ward and Julie flinched. Adam remembered that reaction all too clearly. All your senses on red alert, every moment of the day. Alarm at any sudden noise.

Jenna had leaned forward, her hand tapping Julie's foot gently. 'Hey. Earth to Julie. It's okay, honey, just a porter.'

'Yeah. Just a porter.' Julie's eyes filled with tears and Jenna's helpless gaze flipped to Adam.

'Listen, Julie, these feelings are natural.' Adam repeated what he'd been told so many times. 'It will pass. You just have to hang in there until it does.'

'When?' Julie almost spat the word at him. 'When will it pass?' Adam recognised that sudden, volatile fury too. As if his heart was already full to the brim with anger, and only a drop more would make it spill over.

'I can't tell you. There are ways we can help you…' Adam tailed off as Julie turned her head away from him. He was losing her.

'What do you want, Julie?' Jenna's voice cut across the space between them. 'Dr Sinclair can lie to you if you like. Give you a time and a date when everything will be back as it was. Or he can respect you enough to tell you the truth.'

The warrior was back. The woman who took life by the shoulders and shook hard until she got what she wanted.

Adam grinned and took Jenna's cue. 'I *could* lie. Do you want me to?'

'Of course not.' Julie shot an imploring look at Jenna. 'But it's all so much talk, isn't it?'

Adam saw Jenna's knuckles whiten as she gripped the rail at the end of the bed. She'd done a good job with Julie. She'd gained her trust, and she'd used it to help Iain and the other doctors do their work. But she'd hit a brick wall here.

Unless… Adam hadn't planned on this, but the agonised look in Jenna's eyes spurred him on. 'That's what I thought when the doctors said that to me. So they sent me to a counsellor and I didn't believe her either. In the end you have to find out for yourself.'

He had Julie's attention. Jenna's too, only she was trying not to look at him with such overt interest as Julie. 'What do you know about it?'

'I've been there. Not in the same way as you, but I think I understand part of what you're feeling. I was shot, and ended up in hospital in Florida.'

Julie's eyes were as round as saucers. 'Like on TV?'

Jenna huffed quietly. 'No, it's not the same as on TV, Julie…' Adam waved her to silence. Now wasn't the time for her to spring to his defence, however much it pleased him to hear her do it.

'The thing is that being shot changed my view of the world. Before, I'd thought that I was pretty much unbreakable, but I realised that I wasn't. I had to relearn how to do the smallest things without panicking. But I did, which is how I know that you can. And that you will.'

Julie stared at him, and then gave him a curt nod. Slowly, her eyes left his face and focussed on Jenna. 'Did you bring me some chocolate?'

Jenna reached into her pocket and held up a pound coin.

'It's in the machine if you want it. Dr Sinclair will come with us, it's right outside the doors of the ward.'

Julie fingered the blanket that lay over her legs. 'I don't want to disturb my skin grafts.'

'You won't.' Adam tapped the thick file that he had brought with him. 'I've read all of your notes and the skin grafts have taken nicely. You can get up and move around gently now. In fact, it'll be good for you, stimulate the circulation.'

Julie wrinkled her nose. 'They look horrible. I've seen them when they do the dressings.'

'I know.' He fingered the envelope he had tucked inside the file, wondering whether now was the time to bring it out. 'They'll look better. You know that, don't you?'

'Yeah. S'pose so.' Julie huffed a sigh. 'Every day, in every way it just gets better and better, is that it?'

Adam suppressed a grin. He could see why Jenna had taken to Julie. Underneath all that teenage petulance the kid had spirit. 'Well, yeah. Some days are always going to be better than others, but if you look at it in the long term, things do get better.' He was getting there. He got a grin in return. 'You look better when you smile, you know.'

'Yeah, I've heard that one before too.'

Adam came to a decision and pulled the envelope he had brought out of the file. 'I brought you a picture. One of my patients, I treated her for burns.'

Julie focussed on the envelope. 'So I'm supposed to look at this and see how much progress she's made, am I?' Petulant *and* bright. Adam could see why Julie was such a handful.

'I had a lot of fears when I was hurt. A lot of feelings that I couldn't come to terms with.' The look on Julie's face told Adam that she did, too. 'So did the girl in the picture. It's a tough road, but sometimes knowing that you're not walking it alone makes it a bit easier.'

He was delving much deeper into his own pain than he'd expected to. But somehow, with Jenna sitting quietly beside him, and Julie, whose need was so much greater than his own, it felt okay. Almost a relief.

'Okay. I'll look.' Julie reached for the photograph, struggling to get it out of the envelope with just one hand. Jenna didn't move to help her. Tough love. But it was love, all the same, the kind that was going to haul Julie through this, kicking and screaming if necessary.

Jenna craned over to see the photograph. 'Who's the boy that she's with?'

'That's Rick. They're married now.'

Jenna exchanged looks with Julie. 'He's nice. I think he's more of a Ricky than a Rick, don't you?'

Julie giggled. 'Yeah. Pretty neat guy.'

It wasn't exactly textbook stuff, but it was working. The last thing that Julie was seeing were the faint scars on Claudia's leg. She was seeing a young woman, happy and in love, her handsome boyfriend at her side. Jenna worked round to the scars, but only after she'd made her point about Rick not caring about them. Adam's hand strayed absently to his shoulder. She was almost making him feel better.

'Can you make me a copy of this?' Julie regarded Adam, obviously assessing his age and likely technical competence. 'Do you know how to do that?'

'I've got a copy. Take this.'

'So you like the younger man, do you?' All the way down to the canteen, Adam had been smiling at something, and that was obviously it.

'Oh, go boil your head.' Jenna stuffed her take-away

sandwich into his hand while she rummaged in her bag
for her purse, then grabbed the sandwich back again. She
wasn't best pleased with him, but tact prevented Jenna
from challenging him here and now on the matter.

He shot her a puzzled look and her exasperation began
to cool. Not before he'd noticed it, though. 'Want to talk
about it?' Before she could stop him, he'd taken her sandwich back, showing it to the cashier and then walking
away with it to a quiet spot in the far corner of the canteen.

As soon as she reached the table where he was sitting,
she made a lunge for the sandwich, but he was too quick
for her, holding it out of her reach. 'So you're going to
starve me into submission now, are you?'

'If necessary.'

'I do have money, you know. I can go and get another
one.' Jenna plumped herself down on the chair opposite.

'You're not going to, though.'

She probably shouldn't have shown her hand by sitting
down. 'No. I'm not.' He pushed her sandwich across the
table towards her with one finger, and Jenna took possession of it. 'You might have told me about being shot. That
you know about trauma first hand.' She lowered her voice,
hissing the words across the table at him.

'I might have done.' He rubbed thoughtfully at his
shoulder. 'I would have done, if I'd known that I was
going to tell Julie.'

'That's not the point. Do you really think that you're
best placed to help her if you've still got issues of your
own to deal with?'

'Who says that I do?'

The look in his eyes, for a start. And Jenna was sure
that she'd not been mistaken when she'd thought she'd
heard his stifled cry last night. Even though she hadn't

seen him, she'd sensed his presence out on the patio. 'Well, do you?'

'Not where Julie's concerned. I have it under control.' Maybe he saw the disbelief in her eyes. 'If you want to know, you should just ask. Rob drives me crazy, tiptoeing around what happened as if it's some guilty secret.'

'Well, tact never was Rob's strong point.' She got a grin in response. 'I would like to know, but the canteen's probably not the best place in the world to have this conversation.' Jenna looked around awkwardly.

'It's okay. My fiancée and I were both shot eighteen months ago in Guatemala, in a roadside ambush that went bad. Elena died, and I pulled through. I struggled with it, for a long time.'

The mixed emotions jostling in her chest drained away, leaving only horror and shock. 'Adam, I'm so sorry.'

He slid his hand across the table towards hers, as if he should be the one to comfort her. 'It happened and I won't say that it hasn't changed me. But I'd never let it compromise the welfare of any patient.'

'No.' Her fingers were trembling, and she pressed them down onto the tabletop to steady them. 'I'm sorry, I shouldn't have insinuated that.'

'But I still should have told you?'

'Yes, I think you should.'

He nodded. 'So do I. And I want you to promise me something.'

Anything. She'd do anything she could to help him. 'Okay.'

'If you ever think that a personal issue is getting in the way of my treatment of a patient, you'll tell me. I don't mean dropped hints or concerned noises, but words of one syllable.'

'I can do that. I'm better at words of one syllable than I am at hints.'

He grinned. 'Thought you might be.' He looked at his watch. 'As we're here, do you have time for some coffee?'

'Yes, of course.' Those honest eyes of his. Never once countenancing pity, but demanding respect. Jenna could almost feel them drawing her in, inch by inch. 'I've another twenty minutes of my lunch break left, and they'll page me if they need me.' He went to stand and she beat him to it. 'Stay there, I'll get them.'

Things were beginning to make sense. He'd papered over the cracks of his own trauma so effectively that it only surfaced at night when he couldn't suppress it with an effort of will. And by the time Jenna returned with the coffee, setting his cup down in front of him, he had already moved on and was thinking about something else.

'Acid's a very personal way to attack someone.'

'It was personal. Kind of.' Jenna tipped some milk into his cup. 'Julie has a sister, a year older than her. They're very alike, could be twins. She'd borrowed her sister's blouse and jacket to go out in.'

'And the acid was meant for her sister?'

'Yes. An ex-boyfriend who held a grudge. The parents knew there was a problem there, and had been keeping an eye on Julie's sister.'

'And no one thought to stop Julie from going out dressed in her sister's clothes?' Anger suffused every line of his face.

'Easy to be wise after the event. I've talked to the parents and put in an urgent request for counselling for Julie's sister, but she's not at the top of the priority list.'

He sighed, his finger and thumb massaging the bridge of his nose. 'Do you think it would help if you and I had an informal chat with the whole family?'

Jenna turned the idea over in her head, and decided to trust him. 'Yeah. Yes, I think that would help a lot.'

He'd seemed glad of her company over coffee, and almost relieved when Jenna had steered the conversation round to lighter topics. Relaxed now, he strolled with her all the way back down to A and E, staying to chat to Jenna's colleague Brenda while Jenna went to the locker room. And he was still there when she returned.

'I saw penguins last year when I went to New Zealand. I wasn't too keen on the little blighters but my friend was mad to see them.' Brenda's blond hair, piled up on the top of her head in a messy confection of highlights and lowlights, was shining, along with her smile.

'Yeah?' Brenda had caught Adam's interest and he hardly noticed Jenna's return. 'I'd love to go to New Zealand.'

'Great place. We stopped off in Hong Kong on the way.' Brenda was a seasoned traveller, saving her money and her annual leave for somewhere far-flung every summer. 'I'm planning to go to India this year.'

His arms were folded on the counter in front of him and he leaned forward towards Brenda. 'Are you? Whereabouts?'

Brenda had his full attention now and they were swapping stories about places they'd been, things they'd seen. Jenna didn't have much to contribute to that conversation. Sure, she got itchy feet from time to time, who didn't? But her yearning to see the world had been smothered by the need for security, her home, her career. One day, maybe, she'd have that sufficiently sorted to venture out a little.

'Tell him to come along, Jen.' Brenda was nudging her elbow.

'Uh? Where?' She'd lost track, reckoning that Brenda and Adam were doing fine on their own.

'To the softball match next Friday evening.' Brenda turned her attention back to Adam. 'All the hospitals have teams, and we have a kind of league. We're playing the Marylebone Medics, and they take it all very seriously, you know, practising and not drinking beer until afterwards.' Brenda's eye assessed the full breadth of Adam's shoulders with something more than professional interest. 'I bet you're pretty handy with a bat. We might just stand a chance if I can persuade Rob to play as well.'

'Where do you play?' Adam seemed to be weighing up the offer.

'Hyde Park. Over in the southern section, there's always plenty of room on the sports field to stake a pitch. Our team's the Bankside Cheetahs—because we cheat, not because we resemble a graceful, fast-moving animal.' Brenda giggled. 'Although Jenna has her moments.'

'Right. Like last month when I tripped over your foot.'

'That was just unlucky. Anyway, we're never too proud to welcome a ringer on to the team.'

'I work here. Part time for the next month, anyway.'

'Oh, well, that's even better.' Brenda was scenting victory. 'I thought you were lecturing at the university. They've got their own team but you don't want to be with that lot. Far too young and enthusiastic.'

Adam chuckled. 'I'm filling in with a couple of shifts a week here, as well as working with the reconstructive surgery team.' He grinned. 'We're all sharing knowledge. So, assuming that I'm old and cynical enough for the Bankside Cheetahs, I'm totally legit.'

'Well, that's sorted, then.' Brenda turned her green eyes on to him, full force. 'I was wondering what that orange circle on the roster was. Stands for knowledge-sharing, does it?'

'Guess so.' Adam glanced at his watch. 'But since I'm supposed to be sharing elsewhere today, I'd better make myself scarce.' He gifted Brenda with a devastating smile and nodded at Jenna. 'Later.'

Brenda watched Adam through the automatic doors, chewing speculatively on the end of her pencil. 'How did it go with Julie?'

'Good. He really got through to her. And he was honest with her, didn't treat her as if she was stupid, just because she's young. From what I saw of his case notes at the lecture yesterday, he's an exceptional surgeon.'

'Praise indeed.' Brenda shot a querying glance towards Reception and received a signal that all was quiet. 'So you're practically living with him. What's the story, any lady visitors?'

'Give him a chance, he's only been here two days.' Jenna could see exactly where this conversation was headed. 'You interested, then?'

Brenda shrugged. 'Don't want to step on anyone's toes.'

Jenna shrugged. There was no reason why he shouldn't be dating again. She doubted that Adam was short on offers.

'I wouldn't know. You'll have to ask him. Or Rob, he'd probably know.'

'I didn't mean that.' Brenda was looking at her pointedly.

'Me?' Jenna flushed, shaking her head. 'What are you, mad?'

'What's wrong with that? He's good-looking, seems like a nice guy. Unless you've still got an arrangement with Joe…?'

'Joe? He's been gone nearly a year now.'

Brenda pursed her lips. 'I thought that maybe you were waiting for him or something. You two did seem very cosy right before he left. Didn't strike me as if it was the end of the road somehow.'

Cosy was not the word for it. It had been more like agonised prayer on Jenna's part that a miracle would happen and he wouldn't leave. Or that he'd want her to go with him to Australia. Something, anything other than the harsh reality that he'd just felt like a change of scene and she wasn't included in his future plans.

'No. We split up for good.'

'I'm sorry. I didn't realise, Jen, you seemed so okay with it all that I thought that you two had worked something out.' Realisation dawned on Brenda's face. 'But you were just playing nice, weren't you?'

Jenna shrugged away the hurt. It had been the same when her parents had left, easier to pretend that she didn't care and just get on with her life. 'Joe's ancient history. And Adam's not my type.'

'I would have thought he was pretty much anyone's type.' Brenda shot her a suspicious look. 'But, then, he's not around for long, is he.'

'Exactly. Having one boyfriend leave the country is bad luck. Two looks like carelessness.' Add her parents to the list and it was criminal negligence. Jenna swallowed the thought and grinned at Brenda. 'I could ask you round some time if you're interested, though.'

The idea seemed to appeal to Brenda, but she shook her head. 'No. You know me, I don't run after men. Always better to let them come to you.'

Fair enough. On the evidence of his reactions, Adam might just do that. Brenda was good-hearted, pretty and she knew how to have a good time. No tangled strings. No stupid hang-ups. Just as long as he remembered to close

the French doors at night, if he did decide to take Brenda
up on the offer that Jenna reckoned she was pretty much
certain to make.

CHAPTER FOUR

IT was his fourth night in the flat, and the fourth night in a row that the dream had come. He guessed that it was the change of scene that had brought the dreams back so often. So vividly. Adam gritted his teeth and got on with it. Get out of bed. Shake the dream off. Walk a little and then go back to bed and hope that this time his sleep was untroubled.

The dream clung to him as if he had fallen into a pit of stinking mud. Maybe his talk with Julie and her family that afternoon hadn't helped. It had gone well, but he hadn't been able to get the haunted look in Julie's sister's eyes out of his head.

He padded through to the kitchen and got himself a glass of water, drinking it down in one go. Throwing on jeans and an old T-shirt, he slipped noiselessly through the open French doors and onto the patio to get some air.

'Okay?' Her voice sounded above him, making him jump. Adam wondered whether any of the cries that had sounded through his dream had been real and had woken her.

'Yeah. Warm night again.'

'Yes. I can't sleep.' They both skirted carefully around the real reason for Adam's wakefulness. And perhaps for hers. He'd heard the click of the balcony doors above him more than once these past couple of nights.

Adam sat down on the wide steps of the fire escape. 'Join me?' It was probably a bad idea, but he couldn't help himself. He'd seen her often enough over the last couple of days, but she had seemed remote, less willing to connect with him, and it had chilled him to the marrow.

Her footsteps were silent behind him, but he felt the silky material of her dressing gown brush against his arm as she walked down the steps and sat down next to him. She smelled just lovely. Like an English country garden after a downpour of rain, sweet and clean, with a touch of the deep scent of the earth.

'Is this why you wouldn't stay with Rob and Cassie?' Her voice was quiet, measured. Soothing, like the dark stillness of the night. 'They wouldn't have minded, you know.'

'I do.' The hairs on the back of his wrist were standing on end where the silky material had touched him. The brief sensation had almost made him cry out.

'For Ellie and Daisy?'

'Yeah. The drawing that Ellie did…'

Her soft laugh echoed through his empty heart. 'That was beautiful. Bright colours, smiley faces. It didn't seem like a sad picture to me.'

'To me either. A year ago, six months even, I couldn't have looked at it without breaking down. But now it makes me smile. Elena would have loved it.' He shifted a little, working at the tension across his shoulders. 'This… The dreams aren't for Ellie to know about, though. They're something different.'

'How?'

All he'd wanted these past few days had been for her to challenge him, help him break free of the shackles that were stopping him from doing what all his instincts clamoured for. He'd asked her to be honest with him, speak plainly, and she had. But it wasn't enough.

'I don't want to go there, Jenna.'

He felt her shrink away from him. 'I'm sorry. Fools rush in...'

He was suddenly so sick of this. Sick of the complex dance they'd been doing, never getting too close but unable to keep their distance. 'Angels don't fear anything.'

'I wish I could take a leaf out of their book.'

Maybe he should too. Act as if he was on the side of the angels. Pretend that what he'd told her already was all there was to it, and that there wasn't another part of him that had been irrevocably broken that day on the road.

'Perhaps they should take one from yours.'

She laughed quietly into the moonlight, shaking her head. 'I don't think so somehow.'

Something whispered against his arm, feather soft. The wings of a moth, maybe, or one of the butterflies from her garden, out on a late-night spree. Or maybe it had been a lock of her hair.

'You underestimate yourself. You can teach them a thing or two.' He dipped in a little closer and found that her lips were already there. Euphoria swamped the voice of reason. It would just be one kiss. A man didn't have to fall in love, risk everything again, just for one kiss.

If she'd have stayed still, quiet, maybe he could have resisted her. But he felt her fingers on his jaw, skimming across the night's stubble. Then she whispered his name, and ripped every last thread of his resolve to tatters.

His hands found her waist and she slid onto his lap. He kissed her, heat banking and flaring in his chest until his head began to swim.

'Mmm. That was foolish.' Her lips brushed warmly against his, full of the promise of what he hadn't yet tasted.

'Very.' If the first kiss could be explained away as a heat-of-the-moment thing, the second trashed that particular excuse. They both knew exactly what they were doing. Her gaze locked with his and he was lost, drowning in the deep blue waters of her eyes. Adam poured everything he had, everything he was into the kiss, letting the long, slow beat of their passion take him.

Finally, he let his lips slip from hers and he held her gently to his chest, not caring that she could surely hear the urgent pumping of his heart. She was silent for a long time and when she did speak her voice was almost a whisper. 'Adam, I...'

He rested his cheek against her hair. 'I know. The most foolish things can be the sweetest.'

She laughed quietly and he was glad that he had pleased her. 'Got a little carried away, I guess.'

She knew it wasn't only that just as well as he did. But Adam already cared about her too much to short-change her by taking this any further. 'Yes. Something about a hot summer night. Jenna, I'm sorry if...'

'It's okay. I know.' She hung her head, moving to get up off his lap, but he pulled her down. He may not be able to take this any further, but he wouldn't have her believe what she so obviously seemed to think.

'When I kissed you, Jenna, it was you that I wanted. Just you.'

She gnawed at her lip uncertainly, seeming to be unable to take that fact in. Reality was closing back in on both of them, wrenching them apart, but he couldn't let her go without knowing that these last moments had been special. He dropped a kiss onto the end of his finger, pressing it against her lips, and felt them curve in a smile.

'I suppose I'd better go. Before either of us starts anything we can't finish.' She didn't move from his lap.

'That would be best.' He'd committed himself once to a woman. But that was when he had believed in love without loss. And he had a ready-made excuse not to take this any further. 'I'm only here for a month and then I have to leave.'

'I know.' She seemed almost relieved, as if that had settled some conflict that was going on in her head. A flash of mischief crossed her face. 'Great kiss, though.'

'Yeah. One of the best.' *The* best, as far as he could remember, but saying that would only get him into more trouble than he was already in.

Wordlessly she jumped to her feet, almost running past him and up the steps of the fire escape. Seconds later the click of the door catch above him told him that she had gone straight inside.

He sat for a moment his head in his hands. It was one thing to join forces with Jenna to help Julie, but anything else was out of the question. He was going to have to be very clear on that from now on. Slowly he stood, making his way back through the open French doors, shedding his T-shirt and jeans and throwing himself back onto the rumpled sheets of his bed.

Jenna watched as Brenda shaded her eyes, scanning the park anxiously. 'He said he'd be here. He was tied up with something but he'd definitely be here.' She gave an exaggerated grimace.

'He'll be here, then. Or he won't. One of the two.' Jenna had tried to forget that kiss of a couple of nights ago. Or at least disregard it. It seemed that was what Adam was doing too.

'Well, if he doesn't make it in the next fifteen minutes,

I'll have to put Sue in to bat. And you know how she hates it, she only really comes to watch Andrew.'

Jenna lay back on the rug that was spread under the trees at the edge of the softball pitch. 'I'll go in again. We can do that if we don't have a full team.'

'Yes, but we do have a full team. You can't go twice if we have a full team, those are the rules.' Brenda was stripping the seeds from an ear of wild grass, in much the same way that a vexed child pulled the legs off an insect. 'I suppose we could say Sue's hurt her ankle. Then we wouldn't have a full team.'

'They're all medics too. They can spot a fake injury just as well as we can. You can't fool them with a bandage and some red felt-tip.'

Brenda stared at the opposing team, all dressed in matching sports shirts, huddled together, obviously discussing tactics. 'Yeah, you've got a point. This lot take it all far too seriously, they'd probably want a doctor's note and a second opinion.'

'We'll just have to hope he makes it, then.' Jenna scanned the path leading down from the car park. 'Look, isn't that him there? With Rob?'

'Yes-s-s!' Brenda was already scenting victory and jumped to her feet, waving and cupping her hands around her mouth. 'Come on, you two. Get a move on.'

Adam arrived, was thoroughly chastised for being late, and then sent straight in to bat. Rob sat down on the rug, cracking open a can of beer from the cool box, making exaggerated noises of disgust when the bowler threw a foul ball at Adam.

The next ball was good, and the crack of the bat was accompanied by Rob's roar of approval. The ball whizzed over their heads and Jenna ducked as three fielders from the opposite team thundered past her into the trees.

'Run!' Brenda's screamed instruction was unnecessary as Adam had already dropped the bat and was running. 'No, Erica, don't hang around like that. You'll block him. You run as well.'

Erica obeyed, cantering home just slowly enough to leave Adam stranded behind her on third base. Brenda waved her in to bat, moaning with frustration as a curved ball slipped past her and she was caught out.

'You next, Rob.' Brenda confiscated his beer and pushed Rob to his feet. 'And no daisy cutters.'

'Aren't you supposed to encourage them? You are team coach after all.' Jenna was watching Rob's back as he trudged onto the pitch, picking up the bat.

'I brought the beer, what more do they want?' Brenda watched with approval as Rob took a swing at the ball, sending it off to the corner of the pitch. 'With any luck, they'll clock up a few runs between them.'

By the time Adam and Rob had finished, Jenna and the rest of the Bankside Cheetahs were cheering along with Brenda. Twenty runs, six of them home runs, which more than doubled their score and put them in with a chance.

At half-time Brenda delivered a short inspirational message, which amounted to threats of physical harm if anyone dropped a catch, and then deployed her team, Adam and Rob close in for the weaker batters and in the outfield for the stronger. Jenna was in her usual position at third base, with Brenda herself floating, shouting instructions that no one took a great deal of notice of.

It was a draw. Thanks to a few lucky catches on her own part, some impressive teamwork between Adam and Rob and an almost superhuman catch by Adam, which prompted universal applause. The Marylebone Medics swallowed their incredulity and took it in good part, breaking out their own supplies of beer.

Adam was deep in conversation with one of the opposing team, obviously someone he knew from the way they'd greeted each other. Jenna tried not to watch him, but Brenda had no such scruples.

'Great catch, that. Perhaps we could all practise together next week.'

'Practise?' Jenna's mouth dropped open. 'Since when have we practised? Anyway, getting everyone together for games is difficult enough, what with half the team being on shift at any one time.'

'Suppose so.' Brenda finished gathering the bats and balls together into the large holdall that housed their kit. 'Are you going to take this?'

'Yes, I've got my car with me. Want a lift?'

Brenda grinned. 'No, thanks. That guy from the Marylebone team that Adam's been yacking with all evening lives in my neck of the woods. Adam's going to drop him, and then my place is on the way back to yours from there, so I'll tag along.'

A sour taste suddenly caught in Jenna's throat. So what? It was only a lift. And she'd told Brenda already that she wasn't interested in Adam. One measly kiss wasn't going to change that. Even if it hadn't been one, and if describing the way that Adam kissed as measly was actionable in any court of law.

'Okay. Will you give me a hand over to the car park with the kit, then?'

Brenda helped Jenna to carry the holdall to the car park and dump it into the boot of her car. She could see Adam and Rob strolling forty yards behind them and left Brenda leaning on the bonnet of Adam's car as she accelerated away. Whatever was, or wasn't, going to happen next, she didn't want to be around to see it.

* * *

The next day had dawned bright, clear and, best of all, Saturday. If Jenna had been in the mood to let off steam, and she wasn't saying that she was, then attacking some of the weeds in her butterfly garden would be an ideal way to do it.

She spent some time hacking at the mint, which had run riot across the whole area. Cutting it down and then digging out the network of long, stubborn roots that ran under the soil was hard work, and as the sun climbed in the sky she seemed to get more hot and bothered, rather than less.

'Morning.' She had been tugging at a particularly re-calcitrant root, and didn't hear Adam's approach across the grass. Jenna turned, slipping her gardening gloves off and wiping her forehead as if the redness of her face was due to heat and exertion.

'Morning.' He looked tired and a little bleary-eyed, as if he'd had no sleep last night. Probably hadn't.

'You're working on the garden, then?'

That was self-evident. But, then, if he had any sense of decency, he was just as much at a loss for words as she was. 'Yes. I thought it was time I did some tidying up.'

'Looks like hard work.' His eyes rested on the garden fork, stuck into the earth next to her, as if he was considering offering her a hand.

'It's this mint, it sends out runners all over the place. It's a job to dig it all out.' Jenna grabbed the fork. 'I reckon that's enough for today.'

He nodded, stifling a yawn. If he had the temerity to do that again, she'd probably be justified in stabbing him with the fork. If he stretched then she'd do it slowly.

Jenna looked at her watch. 'Well, I'd better get on. I said I'd meet some friends for lunch.' Let him get back to bed, he obviously hadn't had any sleep last night. Or if he had, it hadn't been here. He'd been quiet enough when he'd slipped in at seven o'clock this morning, but she'd been awake, just as she had been off and on for most of the night.

'Yeah, sure. I just wanted to have a quick chat with you. About last night.'

Oh, no he didn't. It was one thing to kiss. Telling was quite another. And Brenda was Jenna's friend, she didn't want to hear about what had happened last night. Certainly not from him. 'I've got to go.' She looked at her watch again to emphasise that there was no time to stand around talking.

He gave her a questioning look and Jenna gathered up her gloves and fork. 'I'll catch you later.' Much later.

'Sure. Later, then.' He watched her march across the lawn and up the fire-escape steps into her flat. When Jenna tiptoed up to the kitchen window a few minutes later and peered out, he was still standing on the lawn, alone, seemingly deep in thought.

'You look tired. What have you been up to?'

Jenna could well ask the same of Brenda. But instead she pulled her shoulders back and smiled. 'Oh, nothing.'

'And of course today had to be the busiest day since written records began.' Brenda glanced around her quickly. 'I think it's settling a bit now, though.'

'Hope so. Where's Adam? Have you seen him?' Jenna didn't actually want to know where Adam was. She just wanted to know whether the coast was clear to grab a coffee from the machine.

'Booth six, I think. He's been flat out all morning, too.' Brenda peered at her with an air of professional concern. 'You really do look shattered. You need an early night tonight.'

'I'm okay.' Jenna had worked it all out in her head now. About a thousand times. She'd told Brenda herself that she wasn't interested in Adam, and he'd obviously told her nothing to contradict that. She should just keep her head down and not make waves.

Brenda puffed out a breath. 'Catch you for coffee later, then. You look as if you need some. Are you taking the accident victim that's coming in?'

'Yes.' Jenna nodded as the automatic doors to Casualty swished open. 'Looks like he's here already.'

She motioned the porter to take the trolley over to an empty cubicle then turned to the ambulance paramedic. 'What've you got for me, Joel?'

'Young lad, dislocated shoulder that seems to have snapped back into place, bruising around the rib cage. He was thrown off his bike in a three-car pile-up. He was all over the place when we got there, took a swing at Andy before we could get him calmed down and onto a backboard.' Joel shook his head. 'I wish people wouldn't do that.'

Jenna nodded. 'Hopefully it's just the shoulder, then. Has he been breathalysed?'

'Yep. Nothing significant. He's just an aggressive little so-and-so. Watch him, Jenna, his left arm's useless but he's got a handy right.'

'Thanks. I'll keep an eye out.' It happened. People in pain, their systems flooded with adrenaline after an accident. The fight-or-flight instinct kicked in, and the very people who were trying to help got on the end of a fist for their pains. 'You and Andy okay?'

'What, scrawny kid like that? We've seen worse.'

So had she. All the same, Jenna left the door of the cubicle open behind her and stood on the youth's left side, out of reach. 'My name's Jenna and I'm a doctor. I see you're hurt. May I take a look?' She injected what was hopefully the right mix of warmth and firmness into her tone.

'Yeah, okay. Just my arm.'

'All right.' That would do for starters. After that, Jenna would work her way around to giving him a full examination. 'Your name's Peter?'

'How did you know that?' His face was very pale, but two red spots had appeared on his cheeks.

'It's on your notes.' Jenna twisted the clipboard around so he could see the writing and flipped it back again before he could read it. 'Do you have any pain in your neck? Your back?'

'No. I told those idiots in the ambulance. It's my shoulder that hurts. It went out when I came off my bike.'

'Okay.' She reached for the scissors in her pocket. 'I'm going to cut the sleeve of your shirt so I can have a look without hurting you too much. And I really need you to lie still for the moment.'

'Do I get compensation, then? This is a new shirt.'

Jenna refrained from rolling her eyes. If she had a pound for the number of times she'd heard people complain when emergency staff cut their clothing, she'd be a rich woman. 'No, you don't. And, look, it's torn already.'

Peter grimaced at her and allowed her to carefully cut the sleeve of his shirt. The shoulder was red and swollen, but seemed to be back in place. 'It looks as if you've saved me a job. I'll take an X-ray to make sure, but from what the ambulance crew say your shoulder's popped back in again.'

'I don't need any X-ray. I felt it.'

'Well, we need to make sure. And it's important we make sure that you've no injury to your back, as well.' Jenna walked round to the other side of the bed. He wasn't exactly docile, but she couldn't examine him if she didn't get in close. 'Is it okay with you if I take your blood pressure?'

Clearly it wasn't okay. Peter was skinny but strong, and the straps that were intended to immobilise him had left his arms free. When he grabbed the front of her scrubs, pulling her towards him, she couldn't resist him. 'I told you I don't want any of that shit.'

She knew exactly how to hurt him so badly that the last thing he'd be thinking about was grabbing her. Instead, Jenna gripped the edges of the mattress, her nose two inches from Peter's contorted face. 'Okay. Okay, whatever you say.'

'And get me out of this lot.' He'd managed to work free of some of the restraints, and he howled in pain as he tried to use his other arm to get rid of the brace on his neck.

'Peter, stop it. You need to stay still.'

He yanked on her scrubs and her hips slammed painfully against the bed frame. The urge to fight swelled in her chest and she ignored it.

'Let her go. Now.' She couldn't see who was standing behind her, but she knew anyway. Adam's voice was quiet, measured, but as cold as ice.

Peter didn't move.

'Let her go.' Repeat the instruction. Let that be the only thing in Peter's head. His only thought. Jenna took a deep breath.

'Let me go, Peter.' Peter's fingers loosened and she pulled herself free, stumbling backwards with the momentum, feeling Adam's hand on her arm, steadying her.

'Okay?' Those tawny eyes flashed with concern. She didn't want it. She didn't need a knight in shining armour, and even if she did, Adam was the last person she wanted to fulfil that role.

'Yes, fine. Thank you.' She steadied herself, pulling her arm away from him.

Adam ignored her silent plea to leave. He moved in close, between her and Peter, giving Peter a glare that would have cowed a grizzly bear. Maybe, on this occasion, Adam did have something to add to the mix.

'Right.' Adam was firm and clear, brooking no argument. 'You've been hurt and we're here to do what we can about that. What you need to do right now is cooperate and lose the attitude.'

'Or what? The rozzers don't scare me.' Peter's tone of exaggerated defiance gave the lie to his assertion.

Adam let it go and picked up the clipboard containing Peter's notes, scanning them quickly. 'I see you've been breathalysed and you've got some alcohol in your system but not much. Probably from last night. Anything else?'

'Nothing. I'm clean.' Peter cursed Adam comprehensively.

'Yeah, I've heard that one before, but my parents deny it.' The hint of a smile flickered around Adam's lips. 'I can do a drug test if you like, but it's a great deal easier if you just tell me. You can't get arrested for what's in your system.'

True enough. On the other hand, Peter had been driving. Adam had conveniently neglected to mention that. Jenna wondered what he would do if what he obviously suspected turned out to be true.

'Couple of smokes. Last night.'

'Okay. Anything else?'

'Nah. What do you think I am?'

Adam refrained from giving an answer and shot Jenna an amused look. 'Are you happy to examine him now?'

'Of course.' She didn't want Adam waltzing in and taking over. 'If you're busy, I'll call someone else in.'

'That's okay, I'm free for the moment.' He twisted back to face Peter. 'You've got one more chance. Don't blow it.' His glare said it all. Lay one finger on her and you'll have to answer to me.

Jenna didn't much like it, but she knew the rules. You didn't go near a violent patient without someone else in attendance. Peter hardly looked at her as she went about her examination but Adam's looming presence was enough to keep him compliant.

'Any other pain, Peter?' Peter's eyes momentarily flicked to his leg, before he turned on her and snarled in the negative.

'Did your bike roll onto your leg?' That kind of injury was common. Motorbike riders whose legs were crushed when the bike rolled. Peter wasn't old enough to be driving a big machine, but even a smaller one could do a fair bit of damage.

'I said…' Peter stopped short at Adam's warning growl. 'It's okay. Thanks.'

Nothing like a bit of thanks. And this was nothing like it. 'All the same, I'd like to take a look at it, please.' Jenna flipped a look at Adam. Peter was wearing heavy boots, laced up tight around his ankles. She might need some help from him if she was going to avoid being kicked in the face.

'Don't even think about it, mate.' Adam issued the warning and moved to Peter's leg, unlacing one of his boots, taking it off and dropping it onto the bed. When he touched the other foot, Peter's hiss of pain was quiet but unmistakeable.

Adam carefully cut the laces this time, opening the sides of the boot as wide as he could. As he did so, blood plumed over his hands. He reacted quickly, removing the boot, and a deep cut on Peter's ankle gouted blood.

'I need something to put this into.' He was holding the boot away from him, blood dripping from it onto the floor. Peter's thick socks and the tight lacing of the boot had obviously acted like a compress, stopping the wound from bleeding until now.

Jenna moved quickly, grabbing the plastic wastepaper bin, pulling the top off and dumping the liner and its contents onto the floor. 'Here, this'll do.' She held out the bin and Adam dropped Peter's boot carefully inside.

'Don't touch it!' His tone was urgent and when Jenna looked inside the bin she saw the reason for Peter's injury. A small, razor-sharp blade nestled inside the blood-soaked boot and sock. Adam's head swivelled round to Peter, who had suddenly become very pale. 'Okay, mate, you've got a cut on your ankle. All under control.'

Jenna wasn't so sure. He was doing all the right things, but there was something about the look in his eyes, the dead, dull horror when the blood had suddenly covered his hands that set alarm bells ringing in her head. 'Want a hand?'

'I've got it.' His voice was level now. Perhaps she'd been mistaken. 'Can you hand me that gauze, please?' He was still gripping the wound tightly, and taking the gauze pad that she proffered, he quickly slipped it over the jagged cut and reapplied pressure.

The set of his jaw was a little too tight and his eyes had lost their fire. But Adam was a professional, and he never faltered, working quickly to bind the wound and elevate the leg, even taking time to reassure Peter. For the time being Jenna had to allow him a measure of respect. As soon as they were out of this cubicle, she could go back to contempt.

CHAPTER FIVE

'HEY!' Jenna had thought that now Peter's leg had been dealt with, X-rays ordered and a member of the hospital security team was keeping a discreet eye on him, Adam would lay off being stern and commanding. It appeared not.

She turned slowly. Too slowly, as it looked like a comment. So what? It *was* a comment. 'Yes?'

'I want a word.'

'Can it wait?' Jenna looked around her. A and E was currently experiencing one of those lulls between storms, and she could see nothing that required her immediate attention.

'No, it can't. One minute. It's important.'

'The other ambulance from the crash will be here any minute.'

'No, it won't. Brenda says they're still cutting the driver out of the car.'

Jenna pressed her lips together. She didn't want to talk to him, not after he'd found his way into someone else's bed just days after kissing her like that. But it didn't look as if she had much choice. He knew how to act like a professional and she should show that she could, too.

'What can I do for you?' They were in the open area, right next to the nurses' station. What could he say to embarrass her here?

'It's about Julie.'

'What about Julie?' Alarm supplanted resentment in a second.

Adam seemed to relax now that he had her attention. 'She had a bad time on Friday night. She heard that the lad who threw the acid was getting out on bail and she started to panic.'

'Is she all right?' The temptation to run upstairs to Julie's ward was almost irresistible. But Jenna couldn't. It would have to wait. The doctors and nurses there were doing their jobs, and she had to do hers here.

'Yeah. I sat with her, talked it through. When I dropped in on her on Saturday she was much better.'

Jenna swallowed hard. If she'd taken the time to listen to Adam on Saturday, she would have known. She'd had the time to go and see Julie over the weekend, she could have done that.

'I got a page from the hospital just after I left Brenda's on Friday night.' His gaze caught hers and then flipped away again. 'About ten-thirty.'

The significance of the time was not lost on Jenna. She'd driven out of the car park, leaving Adam to take Brenda home at just before ten. It was half an hour's drive to Brenda's. If he'd been back on the road by ten-thirty then he must have just dropped her straight off.

'Ten-thirty.'

'Yep.'

She'd made a mistake. She'd shown that the time he'd got the call was important to her. Jenna tried to gloss over that. 'So you stayed with Julie all night?'

'Yes. How did you know?'

'I heard you come in on Saturday morning.' Joy battled with guilt. Guilt won out. 'I...I should have been there.'

He shook his head. 'Her mother was there. Between

us we pretty much had everything covered. I would have called you if we'd needed you. Julie's okay.'

'Are you sure?' Joy made a late comeback, seeping through her system like an insidious drug.

'She's okay. She's going to be discharged as planned in a couple of days' time. She's doing well.'

'I...I guess I owe you...'

'Yeah, you do.' He broke in before she could offer the apology. 'You owe me a coffee, and I'm collecting after this shift's done.' He looked at his watch. 'Two hours, in the courtyard.'

When he disappeared at the end of their shift without a word to anyone, Jenna knew where he'd be. She found him sitting on one of the benches in the courtyard, his body relaxed and at rest, his eyes scanning the comings and goings around him. Watching the world go by always seemed an active and worthwhile pursuit with Adam.

Jenna sat down next to him, not too close, and handed him the coffee from the cardboard carry-container. 'Oh. Thanks.' He regarded the logo on the cup. 'This isn't hospital coffee.'

'No, I popped out. This is nicer.'

'Yeah, much. Thanks.' He took a sip and leaned back, throwing his arm across the wooden backrest. 'I can do with this.'

'Me, too. Adam, I'm sorry...' This time she got the word out before he stopped her.

'Nothing to be sorry about. You didn't know where I was.' That could be taken two ways. She didn't know that he'd been with Julie. Or that he hadn't been with Brenda.

'I could have given you the chance to tell me.'

He shrugged. 'I could have made you listen.'

He could have. But the tone of his voice told Jenna that perhaps he hadn't fully understood the reason for her attitude until now. 'Anyway.' He obviously didn't want to talk about it anymore. 'I called Patient Services about Peter.'

'Yes, Brenda said.' Jenna had seen Adam talking to Peter again as he'd stitched his ankle. 'They're sending someone?'

'Jake Something-or-the-other. Apparently he's a volunteer but he doesn't stand any nonsense.'

'No, he doesn't. Jake's an ex-fireman, and he's taken on a few kids who are headed in the wrong direction. He's worth his weight in gold.'

'That much? I saw him, he's no flyweight.' Adam chuckled.

'Did you notify the police?'

'Jake said he'd deal with it.' Adam stared out through the high iron railings at the busy street, where two cars had met, bumper to bumper, and neither seemed disposed to back down to let the other through. 'What would you have done if he'd been carrying acid?'

Jenna knew what he was asking. There had been no way of knowing whether Peter had been a victim or an aggressor. Probably a bit of both, that was the way vicious circles started. 'I don't know. I would have let someone else take the decision. Backed out on the grounds of personal feelings.'

Adam nodded. 'That's what I reckoned. Jake's better equipped to deal with it objectively.' The bloody knife had obviously affected him more than he'd said.

'Teenagers are almost always a product of their experience.' If she knew nothing else, she knew that, beyond a shadow of a doubt.

'You think so?'

'Don't you?'

He took another sip of coffee. 'Yeah, I do. Just wondered why you did.'

Her heart was beating a warning tattoo in her chest and Jenna ignored it. This craving for him to know everything about her was probably unhealthy, or at the very least inadvisable, but right now it was impossible to resist.

'I was on that knife edge. When I was adopted by my grandparents, I thought I was alone in the world, and was ready to wage war on everything and everyone.' She shrugged. 'I was only ten, so I didn't get very far. Without them, though, who knows where I would have ended up?'

'You were adopted? My brother and sister are adopted.' He grinned. 'My sister says that Mum and Dad saved her from what she might have become if they hadn't been around.'

'That's it exactly. How old was your sister when she came to you?'

'Five. She'd been through a lot. Lost her mother to drugs. Her father wasn't on the scene.' He shrugged. 'She didn't say one word for the first three months she was with us. She used to tag along after me with this solemn look on her face, clutching this awful old teddy bear.'

'And now?'

'Now you can't shut her up. She graduated from medical school the year before last.'

'What's her name?'

'Mattie.' The look on his face said it all.

'You're very proud of her.'

He chuckled. 'Don't tell her that. But I couldn't love her more if I tried.'

His face was open, full of warmth. So handsome that Jenna could have wept. And he was so close that all she needed to do was to reach out, touch him.

Why did she want him so much? Was it *because* he was leaving? Was she just trying to re-create the pattern she'd been through with her parents and with Joe, somehow make it right this time? Maybe she could make it right this time. Adam was different from Joe in so many ways.

It was too complex a question to consider right now. 'I want to pop in and see Julie before I go home. If you're in tonight, can I give you a knock later?' She made it sound casual, like a friend popping in for coffee. It was, wasn't it?

'Sure.' That smile. The one that left her slightly breathless, as if she'd just run up a flight of stairs. Joe had never made her feel like that, not even in the first bright months of their romance. 'That'd be nice, I'll look forward to it.'

His mistake began to dawn on Adam as he made his way home on the Underground. Just as the crowded train drew out of King's Cross station, he realised that he was smiling. A woman who was crushed against him and trying not to jab him in the ribs with her handbag smiled back and he made an amiable comment on the discomfort of being jammed up in such close proximity to his fellow travellers and looked away.

He hadn't understood Jenna's reaction to him on Saturday, but now he did. And he'd caught himself revelling in the idea that Jenna had been jealous and upset over where she thought he'd been on Friday night. Wondering whether the kiss they'd shared had been so foolish after all.

The train was beginning to empty out at each stop. Adam stood aside and waved the woman next to him into an empty seat. What kind of person took pleasure in another's discomfiture? He did, obviously. And what kind of person acted on it? Well, he could stop himself from doing that, at least.

Fresher, cooler air hit him as he made his way up the steps from the station to pavement level. The walk home seemed to clear his head a little and he dropped his bag in the hall, making straight for the sofa and throwing himself down on it. He was tired. Hadn't slept at all on Friday night, and not much for the two nights since. Slowly, his eyelids began to droop.

Adam tore himself from the grip of a dream of visceral intensity only moments before he heard her knock on the door. Shaking his head, trying to throw it off as best he could, he called to her. 'Just coming. Won't be a minute.'

He took the time to splash some cold water on his face and found her waiting at the front door. She nodded, almost shyly, as he motioned her inside.

'You okay?'

He felt as if the dream was branded across his face. 'Yeah. Sorry, have you been knocking? I fell asleep.' Adam wiped one hand across his face, struggling to dispel the feeling of hollow, aching emptiness.

'Want me to make you a cup of tea?' She was looking at him steadily, frank concern in her eyes.

'No. Thanks.'

She followed him through to the sitting room and sat on the edge of the sofa. 'Adam, please, don't. You're not okay. These dreams…'

He hardly heard what she said for the anger bursting through his veins. Self-loathing at his own deceit. He wasn't some tragic hero struggling through a difficult patch. He was broken, finally and irrevocably, a man who'd failed to do the one thing that he'd promised he would always do, and who had the scars to prove it.

'It's nothing.' His voice sounded harsh, but she didn't flinch. Stared him down with those beautiful blue eyes of hers.

'Pull the other one. It's got bells on it.' Her chin jutted slightly.

'You don't want to go there, Jenna.' He tried to turn away from her but he couldn't.

'Don't tell me where I want to go. That's my decision to make.'

Fine. If that was the way she wanted it. Let her see what kind of man he really was, and then she'd go. Adam caught her hand, pulling her to her feet, and pressed it against his shoulder, knowing that the thin material of his shirt wouldn't disguise the mutilated flesh beneath it.

As soon as her fingertips touched his shoulder, he knew that this was wrong. He let go of her hand, praying that he hadn't hurt her, shaking with guilt and shame.

'Earth to Adam.' She was standing close, her soft voice penetrating the static in his brain, her fingers gently tapping out some kind of call sign on his.

'Are you reading me?' Her voice again. Seemingly miles away but still clear, still something for him to hang on to.

'I read you. I...I'm sorry.' He heard his own voice, broken and weak but trying now to reach out to her.

'Forget the sorry. Just keep this wavelength open.'

He forced himself to take a deep breath. Took a step back, but then the coffee table behind him blocked his retreat, and she moved with him, keeping up the connection. 'I'm sorry, Jenna. I shouldn't have done that. Taken hold of you like that.'

She tossed her head. She may be small, certainly no match for his strength, but she was completely unafraid. Like an angel. 'Let me see them, Adam.'

'You don't want...' He fell silent as her eyes flashed dangerously. She'd already told him about that.

He was unable to stop her as she unbuttoned his shirt, pulling it away from his shoulder. Adam closed his eyes. He'd prefer not to see her reaction. He didn't want to watch and see the same revulsion in her eyes that he saw in his own when he looked into the mirror.

He felt her fingers on his shoulder, cool, gentle like a cleansing balm. Heard her voice, clear and sweet, with no trace of anything but concern. 'Through and through.'

'Yes.' He was speaking almost automatically, powerless to resist her. 'I was lucky. Couple of inches to the right and it would have shattered my shoulder. An inch to the left and it would have hit an artery.'

'Any more?'

He could have said no. Perhaps in some other life, where her candid eyes and soft touch didn't compel the truth from him. Adam unbuttoned his shirt, pulling it free of his jeans and away from the scar beneath his ribs on his right side.

She made no comment but slid her fingers downwards. He sucked in a breath, willing his muscles not to convulse at her touch, his body not to react to her. 'That one they had to dig out.'

'Yes, I can see.' She ran her finger along the small surgical scar that traversed the jagged one made by the bullet's entry. 'Is that it?'

'No.' He sank down onto the coffee table behind him and indicated the line of the red weal that started just above and behind his ear and felt her carefully part his hair so she could see it.

'That one...' She let the sentence drop for an excruciating moment. 'Do you remember anything about what happened?'

'No. Nothing. Elena and I were alone together on the road, and no one really knows.' Hot tears sprang to his eyes and he scraped his hand across his face. 'I don't know if I did anything to help her.'

He heard her breath catch. This final admission, the

one he most hated himself for, had been too much. One step too far. He tried to pull away from her, but she was standing in between his legs and he would have had to physically compel her to move to do so. He'd done that once too often already this evening.

'You don't know that you didn't do anything.'

'I know that I didn't do enough. These road bandits aren't out to kill, they just want to rob. We were travelling in a clearly marked vehicle and they must have known we were aid workers and probably foreign nationals. Something must have gone badly wrong.'

'And you assume that it's your fault.'

'I know that I promised to look after her. And that makes me responsible. Whatever I did or didn't do led directly to Elena's death.'

'I don't believe it.'

Four words. Friends, family had talked with him for hours, telling him all the reasons why he shouldn't blame himself. But those four words, spoken with such certainty, meant more to him than any of it. 'You can't just ignore…'

She could. He felt her arms around his neck, drawing him in, and he pressed his cheek against her body, winding his arms around her waist. For a moment he let himself take the comfort that she offered, and then he gently moved her backwards so he could stand again.

'I want you to go, Jenna.' He needed her to go. Before he did anything that he would hate himself for afterwards. Before he did the unthinkable, and began to fall in love with her.

She looked up at him, tears in her eyes. 'Are you sure?'

'Yes, I'm sure. This can't work for either of us. I'm leaving in three weeks' time.'

He had wondered whether she feared anything and here was his answer. She seemed to retreat back from him, without moving an inch. 'Yes. So you are.' She turned and almost ran out of the room, and Adam heard the door slam behind her.

CHAPTER SIX

ADAM lay in bed, staring at the ceiling, listening to Jenna's footsteps down the stairs and the muffled thud of the front door closing. For the whole of this week he'd been up and out of the house before her and home late, but he'd swapped his Friday shift and had the day off today.

Kicking the tangled sheet away from his legs, he padded through into the bathroom, glaring at himself in the mirror. He didn't much like what he saw. A man who had maintained a cool distance from a woman who deserved more than his polite detachment. She wanted more, he knew that for a fact. And he did, too. Didn't they both deserve the chance to be friends and to let that friendship run its course, wherever it might lead?

He reached into the shower, turning the stream of water on full. If he was going to take that step into the unknown, he may as well do it right. And since doing it right was going to take some effort, he needed to stop messing around and get moving.

It was like déjà-vu, only Adam knew exactly when he had done this last. He was sitting on Jenna's doorstep on a Friday evening, waiting for her to come home. Just as before, he knew exactly when she caught sight of him. That little nervous twitch of her free hand, reaching for her face and then falling to her side. The way she tried not to stare at him but looked anyway.

'Locked yourself out?'

He shook his head, looking up at her. She just didn't know how beautiful she was. 'No. Waiting for you. We've been doing a fair job of missing each other for the last few days.'

She pressed her lips together, her eyes searching his face. Then she smiled. 'Yes. Complicated, isn't it?' She sat down on the step next to him. 'Perhaps we should work out a timetable for the coffee machine. You can take odd hours and I'll take evens.'

'Not going to work. Not unless we include the chocolate machine as well.'

'You don't eat chocolate.'

'You do. And they're right next to each other.' Adam felt the smile working through his bones and breaking through on to his lips. He'd missed her so much. 'Tell you what, you can have both machines any time. I'll go to the one next to Haematology.'

She nodded. 'That's very civil of you.' She was fiddling with the strap of her handbag. 'Or I suppose it wouldn't do any harm if we acted like adults.'

'You mean share the same drinks machine?'

She shrugged. 'As long as we're not too obvious about it.' She was starting to relax and her tiredness seemed to lift as she did so.

'I don't want to leave things this way, Jenna. I wish we could be friends.' He'd said it and there was no going back now.

She smiled up at him, that tense, slightly worried smile that she gave when she was thinking. 'We are friends. It just seems that there are an awful lot of rules to it at the moment.'

'Is that what you want?'

'It strikes me that putting limits on a friendship rather defeats the object.'

'Me, too. Can I admit to having broken the rules today, then?'

'What, you went to my coffee machine?'

'Worse than that. Want to come and see?'

She hesitated. He gave her an encouraging smile, and the investment yielded a massive return when she grinned back at him. 'Okay.'

She followed him around the house and through the side gate. Her little cry of astonishment made all of the sweat and the blister on his hand worth it. 'Oh! Adam!' She stopped short, one hand flying to her mouth.

'Like it?' He turned, grinning. He'd done the best job he could, weeding and tidying up her butterfly garden, finding the patterns of the original planting and restoring them.

'No, I love it. Thank you.'

'I got you some things to plant as well, to fill in a few of the gaps.' He gestured over to the tubs on the patio. Pink and white lavender to complement the blue she already had. Hebe. Lilac.

For a moment he thought she was going to hug him, but instead she dropped her bags and ran over to the tubs, bending down to take in the scent of the flowering plants. She had lost all of the weariness in her step and was laughing with delight. 'You must have spent all day on this.'

Pretty much, but her reaction rewarded him ten times over. His heart beat a little faster as he moved on to his next piece of rule-breaking. 'Are you too tired to come out for a spot to eat?'

She hesitated again, just long enough to make it seem like a victory when she nodded. 'I am quite hungry. Where did you have in mind? Most of the places around here are packed on a Friday evening.'

'I know somewhere that won't be. It's quiet, just the two of us, and we can…' What? Adam deliberately hadn't thought that far yet. It needed the two of them to decide what happened next. 'We can talk.'

'I'll, um… Can you give me fifteen minutes, just to take a shower and get changed?'

His heart practically jumped into his throat. He hadn't realised how very much he wanted this until she'd said yes.

'Do I need to bring anything special? Wellington boots? Sun hat? Sou'wester and a pair of walking shoes?'

He laughed. 'No. Just bring yourself.'

He still wouldn't tell her where they were going. He drove north, and in thirty minutes they were on an open road, houses and shops behind them and countryside ahead. 'It's nice to be out of town once in a while.' Jenna was watching the sun slanting across the fields and wondering whether she could do that warm light justice if she tried to paint it.

'I thought you might like to get out of town for a change.' He glanced across at her. 'You look nice tonight. Very retro, it suits you.'

'It's not really retro.' Jenna smoothed the skirt of her dress across her legs. 'This is one of my grandmother's dresses. She had loads of clothes that she didn't wear any more, all in storage. She got a lot of them cut down for me, because I liked them so much.'

She was pleased he liked the dress. She liked it too, and she'd worn it for a reason. Live for today, Grandma had always told her. And tonight she had an opportunity to listen to that advice.

He chuckled. 'So that's a genuine Horrocks summer dress.'

'Yes. How did you know?'

'One of my sisters went to the London College of Fashion. She loves vintage clothes and I've learned how to tell one label from another over the years.'

'Really? You'll have to ask her over sometime, I've still got a load up in the attic. Gran was always very well dressed.'

He laughed. 'It's a nice offer, but you don't know what you're letting yourself in for. Ask one and you're likely to get flattened in the rush when they all turn up.' His eyes twinkled with amusement. 'And I won't be able to save you.'

'How many sisters do you have?'

'Oh, there's a whole gang of them. Five at the last count, and a brother.' He laughed at her stifled gasp. 'Christmas is always interesting.'

'It must be…' His tone told her just how it must have been, growing up in such a large family. Warm. Loving.

'Noisy. It's pretty noisy when we all get together. And now that three of my sisters are working on grandchildren, it's even noisier.' He chuckled. 'My mum loves it. My dad keeps threatening to move out for a bit of peace, but it's just bluster.'

'So where do you come in the pecking order?'

He grinned. 'I have two older sisters, Nell and Sophie, then there's me, then Rachel and Caroline who are twins and then my brother Jamie, and Mattie, who's the youngest.'

Jenna was struggling to get her head around him being one of seven. 'So your parents had five children, and then adopted two more?'

'Yeah. Gluttons for punishment, my mum and dad. But we all looked after each other quite a bit.'

'You must think my house very strange and silent.' The admission just popped out before Jenna had time to think about it.

'It's...different. I like it, though. You've filled it with life—your art, your garden.' He grinned. 'Anyone with six siblings gets to know the value of silence.'

'Stop it. You wouldn't be without them.'

'No, you're right, I wouldn't.' He flipped his eyes towards Jenna for a moment and then back on to the road. 'Mattie's a lot like you.'

'I guess I should take that as a compliment.'

'It is. To both of you. If it's okay to compliment you, that is.'

Tonight she'd let it pass. 'I'd like to meet her.'

'Yeah, she'd *love* to meet you. She's been nagging me for a while now about dating.'

'Oh, so this is a date, is it? You might have told me.'

He flashed her a wicked grin. 'Well, I've got a clean shirt on. We're on our own in the car and I'm taking you somewhere nice. You look gorgeous. Go figure.'

'Where *are* you taking me?' The bit about looking gorgeous wasn't lost on Jenna but she decided to let that pass, too.

'It's a surprise date.' Adam slipped out of the fast lane, slowing as he approached the junction to exit the motorway.

'I'm surprised already.'

'Ah. Well, hold on to your hat, then. What do you say we...? Huh. What do you say we just go round this roundabout again? I've missed my exit!'

Jenna kept silent, letting him concentrate on driving until they were on the right road. By the time they were, he'd obviously thought better of whatever it was that he'd been about to say. *What do you say we leave the ghosts behind, just for tonight?* Maybe. *What do you say we stop trying to ignore the past and think about the future?* Maybe. *Wouldn't that be nice?* Wouldn't it just.

They drove through a couple of small villages, and then Adam turned off the road, pulling up outside a gate and jumping out of the car. Ignoring a sign that said that the land beyond was private, he swung the gate open, and they bumped along a mud track that seemed to lead to the middle of nowhere.

'Is this it?' Jenna was starting to wonder whether a dress had been the right choice of attire for the evening.

'Nearly.' He shot a grin at her. 'You won't get it out of me, you know. I want to have the pleasure of surprising you.'

It was a pleasure, was it? Warmth flowed through her veins, like molten gold. Jenna drew her arms across her body, hugging herself as they drove up a steep incline, to the top of a hill that was crowned by a knot of trees.

He drew to a stop and jumped out of the car, opening her door. Jenna got out, stretching her limbs. The view was magnificent. She could see for miles across fields and woodland, dotted with houses and small villages. It was breezy enough that she was glad of the thin cardigan she had slung around her shoulders, but the wind was still warm from the heat of the day. 'This is lovely.' She took a deep breath. 'Just the thing to blow away the cobwebs.'

He grinned. 'And we're not even there yet.'

He took her hand and led her through the canopy of trees. Up ahead there was a wall, old bricks, weather-beaten and worn, which seemed almost as much a part of nature as the trees around her. She strained to see what was beyond it, but it was too high.

'Close your eyes.' He'd come to a halt by a carved wooden door, cut into the wall, and pulled a set of large, old-fashioned keys from his pocket.

Jenna obeyed, placing one hand over her eyes and hanging on to Adam's shoulder with the other. He'd brought her to some mysterious, magic place and she shivered with expectancy. She heard the sound of a key turning in a lock, and then Adam's hand on her waist guided her carefully ahead.

There was the sound of a door creaking closed behind her. She could smell lavender, and when something brushed on her cheek she reached out to touch it. 'Lilac.'

'That's right.' His voice was quiet, almost a whisper, and she could feel his breath on her ear. He took her another couple of steps, positioning her just so, as if he wanted her to get exactly the right view. 'You can look now.'

Jenna opened her eyes, clinging on to him still. In front of her was a round structure with a domed roof and old stone steps leading up to an arched doorway. Flower beds radiated out from it, in concentric circles, criss-crossed by paths made from weathered brick paviours. The whole was contained by a high wall, one side of which she'd seen from the outside.

'Adam! This is beautiful. What is this place?' It was like a magical secret garden, deep in the countryside. If a unicorn had appeared from somewhere and ambled up to nuzzle her hand, she would hardly have been surprised.

'It belongs to my uncle. He owns this land and when he bought it the observatory was up here, pretty much in ruins. It's taken him twenty years to restore it, and the garden.'

'But what was it doing here?'

'This land used to be part of an estate connected to a

big country house. This was the lord of the manor's own private observatory.' He grinned. 'A rather extravagant version of a garden shed, where he could leave the house behind and do his own thing, I guess.'

'And your uncle did all this himself?'

'Pretty much. Dad used to bring us here a lot in the summer when we were kids, and he worked on it with my uncle. See that brick path over there?' He indicated the line of one of the paths that traversed the garden. 'All my own work. A little rough in places, but I was only fourteen.'

'So this place must be special to all your family.'

'Yeah. It's very special. Come and see the observatory.' He led her through the garden and up the stone steps, unlocking the door and opening it for her. 'It was pretty much a shell when he came here, but Uncle Jim's restored it back to its original use. With a few modern twists.'

In the gloom Jenna could see an upholstered bench running the full circle of the smooth, painted walls. A set of comfortable chairs indicated that here stargazing was not a solitary pursuit. And above her head, suspended by a system of pulleys and supports, was a telescope.

'Shade your eyes.' Jenna obeyed without comment. He seemed to have this worked out, to the last step, one delight after another. Adam operated a large wheel by the door, turning it with ease.

'Adam!' Jenna stared, open-mouthed. The panels of the dome had rolled to one side, leaving only glazing on three of the four sides, and the whole space was flooded with light. She saw cream-painted walls, rich, russet-coloured upholstery and, nestling in the curve of the ceiling, the gleaming telescope. 'How did the roof roll back like that?'

'It's all done with smoke and mirrors.' He grinned.

'My uncle's an engineer by trade, and he spent years designing it all and getting it working.' He pointed upwards. 'You can let the telescope down to a comfortable viewing height when night falls.'

He gave her a chance to wander around, his eyes following her as she ran her hands over the large wheels that rotated the dome, sat to admire the comfort of the chairs, and stood at the centre of the compass pattern in the mosaic floor to stare at the sky above her head.

'So.' He finally rubbed his hands together in a sign that there was more to come. 'Do you want to eat first or see the garden?'

Food. He'd thought of everything. 'Oh. Well, I'm hungry, but I want to see the garden while it's still light.' Smell the scents of the evening before dusk fell.

'Both, then.' He chuckled. 'That's fine. Go outside and have a look around and I'll join you in a minute.'

Adam shooed her away and busied himself on a small paved area at the back of the observatory, carrying out a couple of chairs and fighting with a fold-up table. Left with nothing to do, Jenna wandered the garden, smelling the herbs and flowers.

The whole place was full of little individual touches. One corner planted with medicinal herbs. An old stone bird bath with butterflies, birds and a tiny mouse carved amongst leaves and flowers. Jenna was inspecting it, running her fingers along the pitted surface, when a loud pop made her jump.

'Watch out!' he called. Something thudded against the wall twenty yards away, and Jenna ran to retrieve it. 'Sorry about that. Must have shaken it up a bit.' Adam was grinning at her, holding a foaming champagne bottle in one hand. 'Care for some very fizzy champagne?'

While she'd been immersed in the garden, he'd laid

the table. Crisp white linen. Glasses, plates and heavy, old-fashioned cutlery. By the side of the table was an ice bucket.

'Where on earth did you get all that from?' Jenna had been expecting a sandwich and vacuum flask.

He laughed. 'The bench in the observatory is actually cupboards. Jim's latest addition is a solar-powered fridge. Sit down.' He poured two glasses of champagne and handed her one. 'What shall we drink to?'

There was no tomorrow to drink to. Or, at least, not too many of them. 'Tonight. Let's drink to tonight. It's perfect, Adam, thank you.'

He smiled, meeting her gaze, and she was locked into the pleasures of the moment. Forget yesterday. Forget tomorrow. Now was too good to spoil with their corrupting decay.

'Tonight, then.' He tipped his glass against hers and she was lost.

He'd brought food—salads, cold meats, crusty bread, which he produced in succession while they talked and ate, enjoying the cool colours and scents of the garden. As dusk fell, and colours faded to grey, he lit a lantern, which shone a pool of light onto the table.

'So where is your uncle, then?'

Adam laughed. 'Friday night is dance night.' He leaned across the table confidingly. 'He's got a lady friend down in the village. He won't be back home until late, if at all.'

'That's a shame. I'd have liked to thank him.'

His lips twisted in a wry grin. 'You can put a note through his letterbox—we passed the house at the bottom of the hill there.' He took the keys from his pocket and dropped them into her hand. 'We've got this place to ourselves tonight. So as soon as it's dark enough we can do a little stargazing, if you'd like.'

'I'd love it. Strawberries first, though.'

'Of course.' He picked up one of the large strawberries from the dish between them and held it under her nose.

'Mmm. Love the smell of strawberries.' She took a bite. 'And the taste.'

He leaned towards her, dropping the strawberry onto the white tablecloth. 'Love your smell.' He moved closer, and Jenna leaned to meet him. 'And your taste.'

The kiss was a feather-soft sensation on her lips. There was no way he could get any closer to her as the table was between them. For a moment Jenna thought he would sweep it away with one bold stroke and take her in his arms, but he didn't. Even so, he lingered, stretching towards her, his fingers light on her jaw.

'I'm breaking the rules again.'

Jenna smiled at him. 'You don't seem very contrite about it.'

'Maybe they don't apply up here.'

'So we're lost in uncharted territory.' The earth had turned and the sun had slipped beneath the horizon. 'We'll just have to do whatever feels right.'

'Don't tempt me, Jenna.' His eyes were dark, soft pools of shadow that held unthinkable pleasures.

'Would you give in?' He'd give in. She knew he would. If only for tonight.

'When an irresistible force meets an immoveable object...'

'And you're immoveable, are you?'

'Which makes you irresistible.' He brushed her lips again and Jenna's insides turned to jelly.

She put one finger across his lips and they formed into the shape of a kiss. 'So what about the laws of the universe? Do they apply up here?'

'Maybe.' He smiled at her. 'Shall we check them out?

See whether the stars are still where they're supposed to be?'

He carried the lantern into the observatory, holding her hand all the way. It was like being a teenager again. Holding someone's hand in the dark, feeling the thrill of what might or might not happen next. The cautious slide into the unknown. It was as if Joe didn't exist and Adam was the first man who had ever kissed her.

Jenna watched as he heaved on the controls, bringing the telescope down to a comfortable height for viewing and opening a panel in the ceiling to the night air. He consulted a chart and pulled again on a different wheel, this time expending more effort on it, the muscles in his shoulders swelling to take the strain as the dome above her head swung round.

He showed her the moon, bright, filling the lens completely, large craters now plainly visible. Saturn and its rings, low in the evening sky. Then he showed her the stars, naming each one for her. Albireo, at the head of Cygnus, the swan, which the telescope showed to be a bright double star. Vega in Lyra, Corona Borealis. Magical names, which seemed to fit right in with the enchantment of the night.

When she began to shiver, he wrapped a woollen throw around her shoulders. When she exclaimed with the wonder of it all, he seemed to draw closer, caught up with her in the marvels of the universe.

'Let's go home.'

'Yeah? We can get a glimpse of Mars and Venus on the horizon just before dawn, if we're lucky.'

Jenna twisted in his arms, brushing a stray lock of hair away from his forehead. 'Not good enough. I want more than a glimpse.'

He gazed at her, and suddenly she felt as if she were

the centre of the universe. Drawing everything around her inwards by some fluke of gravity. 'Are you sure, Jen? This is… Some stars align only once. In our lifetimes, anyway.'

'I know. Is that a reason for us not to take our chance when they do?'

His arms tightened around her. 'Not for me. I want to write your name and mine across the sky tonight. But when I go, I won't be back.'

That was unlikely. Adam had family, friends here, but that wasn't what he meant. He wouldn't be coming back for her. But at least he was honest about it, and wouldn't leave her agonising over hollow promises to return. 'I know. But tonight we can do as we please. The stars don't care, they'll keep turning without us for a while.'

He kissed her. Long and slow. Earth-moving. She'd found her way back from his last kiss, but this one took her way beyond any possibility of retracing her steps.

'Whatever the lady wants…' He'd already taken the leftovers from their meal to the car, and all he needed to do was stow the telescope back in place, close the overhead window to the heavens and lock the door. Then he caught her hand, leading her through the darkness of the garden.

They hardly touched, hardly spoke. Only his fingers, twined with hers, told Jenna what she needed to know. That he was there still. And that for the moment he wasn't going anywhere.

It was one in the morning, and the drive back to town took less time than the drive out, the dark streets almost empty of cars. It was as if they were in their own small world, not needing anything else. Just being here, with him, was the only thing that Jenna wanted, and she ignored the minutes ticking away on the dashboard clock. It would end. But not right now. Not yet.

CHAPTER SEVEN

SHE had her back against the door of his flat. Nothing mattered, not how she'd got here or what she was going to do next. She felt nothing other than his kiss.

When he had finished kissing her mouth, he moved to her jaw, and her neck. 'Your place or mine?' He hardly stopped to voice the question.

'Mine's too far.' Her legs had gone to jelly and she doubted if she'd make the stairs without help.

The door gave behind her. Somehow he'd had the presence of mind to get the key out of his pocket and slide it into the lock while still kissing her. Without its support Jenna almost stumbled backwards, but his arm around her waist steadied her, pulling her into the safety of his body.

He backed her through the door, kicking it closed behind him, and pinned her against the wall of the hallway. His keys jangled unnoticed onto the floor, along with the bag from the all-night chemist, and now that both his hands were free, he made the best use of them.

One hand was behind her head, and the other... The other explored her body, waiting for each breath that she caught, each quiver of her muscles to tell him which way to go next.

He kissed her throat, bending just enough to cup his free hand behind her leg, pulling it gently upwards until the fabric of her dress tangled around his thigh. A little pressure, the smallest friction, through folds of cloth and Jenna felt her body arch into him and she threw her head backwards, crushing his fingers against the wall.

'Oh! Sorry…your fingers…'

'That's okay, I've got another hand.' That other hand had finally found its way through her skirts and his fingers were sliding along the skin of her thigh.

She was trembling in his arms. Waiting. Waiting, with every nerve screaming for what came next.

'Tell me what you want.'

That was the one thing she hadn't expected. 'I…I… You.'

His low chuckle reverberated against her neck. 'Mmm. I want you too, honey. But that's not all I want.' His lips found the sensitive spot behind her ear, making her shiver. 'I want to know how I can please you.'

His voice was low, insistent. No one had ever asked that of her before, and his point-blank demand melted a shard of ice that had been embedded in her heart for so long that she hardly even knew it had been there. There was nothing she needed to do or say to make him want her. She just needed to be, to feel.

Jenna clung to his shoulders as if he were the most precious thing in the world to her. At this moment he was the only thing in the world. His mouth was on hers again, his hand sliding from the back of her head to her breast, his fingers caressing gently.

He tore a sigh from her throat and then a cry. Not satisfied with that, he slowly stepped up the pace until she choked out his name.

'Do that again. Please.' Was it really her saying these things?

'You mean…this?' His eyes blazed bright, and she no longer cared. She just wanted Adam's hands on her.

'Oh! Yes.' Her fingers found his belt and she tugged at it. 'Bedroom.' There was only one thing on her mind right now, and that involved a bed. And Adam. Not necessarily in that order.

'I like the way you think. But I won't let you out again. Not until…' He let the sentence drift, floating through a myriad of possibilities, each one of them more delicious than the last.

'You asked me what I wanted.'

'So I did.' He lifted her up and carried her into the bedroom, sitting her gently down on the bed and kneeling before her. He stripped off his shirt as if he couldn't wait to be rid of it. No hesitation, no trying to hide his scars. Just for tonight they didn't seem to exist, either.

He was more beautiful than she could have imagined. Sun-burnished skin and lean, finely muscled lines. She looked, and then touched. Then kissed. His skin was smooth, warm and she could almost taste his desire.

'Now you.' He was easing her out of her dress, his mouth and tongue exploring as his fingers exposed more flesh.

'So beautiful.' She was naked now, and his fingers trembled against the sensitive skin of her neck. 'I can hardly bear to touch you, you're so beautiful.'

'Tell me you're kidding.'

He laughed, rolling her back onto the bed, his body covering hers. 'Yeah. I'm kidding.'

The man that Jenna woke up with was a stranger. One who had slept peacefully in her arms. One who had made love as if he had been hungry for life, drinking in every last blissful drop of her pleasure and his own. And there had been a lot of pleasure. He'd made quite sure of that. Adam's eyes flickered open and focussed lazily.

'Hey, honey.' There was no trace of regret. No second thoughts in his golden eyes as he wrapped his arms around her more tightly, pulling her into him. 'What are you doing?'

'Watching you.' The night had been warm and at some time while they'd slept the sheet that covered them had been thrown aside. In the chill hours before dawn his body had kept her warm.

'What do you see?'

She nudged at his shoulder. 'Stop fishing for compliments. You know what I see.' In the end, she'd told him everything. What she wanted. How good it felt when he gave her everything that she dared to ask for, and then more.

'Oh. Can't I have just one? I'll make you a cup of tea.'

'In that case, you can have as many as you like.' She disentangled herself from his limbs, pushing him towards the edge of the bed. 'When you come back.'

He chuckled, pulling her towards him for one last kiss and, too late, Jenna realised her mistake in letting him get out of the bed they'd shared. It was too tender, too full of emotion to be just a kiss. It tasted like the beginnings of a goodbye.

Inch by inch he was leaving her. He had gone into the shower naked and entirely hers. Come back out again with a towel tied around his waist, another draped around his neck, hiding the scars on his shoulder. If his dreams were like an evening mist, dissolved under the heat of a new day, then so was the man who could forget about the past and the future.

But his smile remained. All the way through breakfast,

and as they walked together to the local shops to catch the last few hours of the farmers' market that set up in the station car park every Saturday.

'Which way now?' Adam had two heavy string bags slung over his shoulder and was working on lightening the one that Jenna carried by dipping into the bag of apples he'd bought.

'Do you mind if we drop into the library?' Jenna pointed to the large old building, just along the street.

He shook his head and began to amble along the road. 'Can I carry your books home?'

She laughed. He made everything so easy. No rush, but at the same time he seemed to get an enormous amount done just by moving steadily from one task to the next. 'If you like. Perhaps I should get some talking books, they're not so heavy.'

'Spoilsport. How am I going to earn a big thank-you for lugging four CDs back home?'

'You'll have to use your ingenuity.' She liked Adam's ingenuity. Very much.

His low chuckle drifted in her direction. 'Racking my brains as we speak.'

They climbed the stone steps to the impressive Victorian building, and walked through a pair of glass doors to an old-fashioned reading room. He waited while Jenna took her talking-book CDs from her handbag and handed them to the woman behind the desk for scanning. 'Is there a community noticeboard here?'

'Yes, over there. Why, thinking of joining a club?'

'No.' He had taken the last bite of the flesh of his apple and was working his way through the core, leaving only the stalk. 'Remember the kid with the knife in his boot? Peter?'

'Of course I do.'

'I made a bet with him. If I don't come up with the goods then I owe him a tenner. And since I'm pretty sure I know what he'll spend it on, that's not going to happen.'

'You think we'll ever see him again?' Jenna had heard from Jake that Peter hadn't turned up for his appointment with him, and that he wasn't answering his calls and texts either. 'What's the betting he's back doing all the things he's always done? Carrying a knife. Drinking, taking drugs.'

Adam shrugged. 'No reason to give up on him.'

'You'll have to. You can't keep chasing him from Florida.' The word no longer evoked images of sun and the ocean. It was the word that reminded Jenna that Adam didn't live here, and that soon he'd be going home.

'True.' He seemed to be considering the implications, too. 'But that's something I can't do anything about. I won't give up on him until I have to.'

Right. He couldn't see that moving around as he did was a choice. That making connections and then leaving them behind was part of that choice. Jenna let the thought slide. 'So what's this bet about?'

'He bet me I couldn't come up with a list of fifty things you can do on a Saturday night for a fiver. I'm up to thirty-nine and I'm running out of ideas.' Last night's mischief flashed in his eyes and Adam crowded her backwards in between the shelves of books until they were out of sight, then captured her against him, pulling another apple out of the bag she was carrying.

'Is scrumping one of the thirty-nine?' Florida was suddenly a million miles away and his body next to hers was all that mattered.

'No. Good thinking. That can be number forty.'

They strolled home, discussing the leaflets for clubs and courses that Adam had picked up at the library, then made something to eat. Adam had some work to do for his lecture the next day and he brought his laptop out into the garden, sitting with Jenna under the sprawling oak tree that shaded the far end of the lawn.

Afternoon turned to evening, and Adam snapped his laptop shut, dozing in the shade, while Jenna sketched. When she laid her pencil down, he sat up and stretched. 'Would you like to plant those shrubs?' He indicated the plants he had brought her, still on the patio in their tubs.

'Yes.' She contemplated the butterfly garden. 'Where do you think they should go?'

'Oh, I'm leaving that to you. You're the one with the artist's eye. I'll just do the digging.'

He hauled the tubs down to the edge of the lawn, and Jenna indicated the positions she thought they'd look best in. Smiled when she changed her mind. Chuckled quietly when she changed it back again and apologised awkwardly.

'That's okay. I could do with the exercise. This easy life in London's making me fat and lazy.'

'Fat where?' She ran her fingertips across his hard, flat stomach.

He laughed out loud, pulling her into his chest. 'That's for you to find out.'

She took the bait and ran her fingers across his arms, his back. 'Still looking.'

'Keep going.' He kissed her full on the lips. Could she hope for tonight? Jenna had thought not, but as the sun had fallen, he'd seemed to lose the inhibitions of the day. It would be dark in a couple of hours, and the part of Adam that was wholly hers seemed to have woken, stretching and yawning after a day's slumber.

'I thought you were meant to be digging.'

'Determined to make me sweat, eh?'

'Absolutely.' She nestled into his neck, standing on tip-toe on the broken earth. 'Love the smell of your sweat.'

'Pheromones. You like my smell, I like yours. Mother Nature does the nicest things sometimes.'

Was that all it was? The chemistry of attraction? There seemed to be so much more between them than that. Chemistry blew those thoughts from her head as Adam ran his hand down the full sweep of her back, and she clung to him, pressing her body against his.

'There's always payback, though.'

The word struck cold into her heart. 'What payback, Adam?'

'You make me sweat and I'll make you...' he brushed his lips across her forehead '...glow.'

That kind of payback she could handle. 'Seems fair enough. What else?'

'Wait and see.' He drew back a little, his golden eyes dancing playfully. 'Go and get the spade, and we'll get these planted first.'

Adam dug four deep holes, and Jenna fetched some compost from the bag he'd left on the patio. Together they lifted the plants from their tubs into the ground and Adam shovelled earth around them. When they'd watered them well, Jenna went into the house to fetch a drink and when she returned found Adam back under the oak tree, reclining on the cushions.

'Thanks.' He took the glass from her and drank deeply. 'You'll have to change your sketch now.'

He hadn't touched her sketch pad but it lay open on the rug beside him, her drawing of the butterfly garden plainly visible. 'No, I'll do another. That was how it was at that moment in time. I felt differently about it then.'

'Oh? How?'

She shrugged, sitting down beside him. 'I'm not sure.

Everything changes, moves on from moment to moment. What you see depends on how you feel.' When she'd made that sketch she'd wanted to preserve her memories of yesterday. She hadn't included any of the promise that she now felt for tonight in it.

He nodded slowly. Picked up the leaf of the pad and looked at the next page and broke into laughter. 'So this is how you see me, eh?'

She'd drawn him in cartoon, covered in mud, chasing after a small boy who dribbled a football out of his reach. Jenna bit her lip. Perhaps he wouldn't like it. He might not like the other one either where he was pressing a stethoscope to the furry chest of a small bear, sitting on a bench in a queue of children and adults. 'Just playing around. I got the ideas from some of the pictures you showed at your lecture.'

He was grinning broadly. 'I think they're great. Can I have a copy?'

'Take that one.'

'Thanks. Will you sign them for me?'

'They're only cartoons.'

He rolled over towards her, catching her hand and pressing her knuckles against his lips. 'They're wonderful. Stop underestimating yourself.' He picked up her pencil and pressed it into her hand. 'I want them signed.'

Jenna pretended reluctance as she quickly initialled both portraits, tearing the sheet from the pad and giving it to him. Too late she remembered the drawing that was beneath it.

'Is that how you see me, too?' Alarm flashed in his eyes as he saw the drawing.

There was nothing wrong with the portrait. Adam, asleep under the oak tree, his face relaxed and contented. It was just how he had looked. But seeing it again, Jenna realised that she'd given too much away. There was love in every line of it. Raw longing in each smudged shadow.

She shrugged and put the pad to one side, flipping it closed. 'Kind of.' Her stomach was turning now. If he hadn't seen it in the drawing, he must see it in the blush that was spreading across her cheeks.

He nodded slowly, as if he was turning something over in his mind. 'Jen, last night...'

He was going to say it. Last night had been a mistake. She'd thought he might say it all day, but this evening had chased those fears away. The world had turned again, though, throwing them back to where they'd started out. 'Last night was incredible. It'll always stay with me, wherever I go.'

She suddenly felt sick. If anything, that was worse. 'Yeah... Me, too.'

'I have to leave, Jen. You know that.'

She didn't know anything of the sort. He had a choice, and leaving was what he'd opted for. 'There are people there who need you.' The words almost choked her.

'I've been wondering if...maybe you'd like to come out to Florida. For a holiday. I'd love to show you around.'

She almost punched him. Instead she pretended to think about the offer. 'Perhaps. I'd rather go to South America. See the work you do there. Perhaps even help out a little.' If he went for that, she might just consider it.

'No.' The one sharp interjection pierced that particular bubble before it had even started to float. 'I...I don't think that's a good idea, Jen. It's no place for...' He broke off. 'Don't ask me to take you there.'

'Then don't ask me to come to Florida.' She had thought she could do this. Thought that honesty and certainty would make things all right. But that had been before he had shown her that lovemaking was so much more than just the joining of two bodies.

'But, Jen...' He broke off in exasperation. 'I don't see the difference.'

'Let me tell you the difference, then.' It was either rail at him or burst into tears at this point. Or both. 'My biological parents are Alexis and Daniel Thorn. They're alive and living very nicely, thank you, in the South of France.'

She'd shocked him into silence. Tears were coursing down her cheeks and Jenna rubbed angrily at them with her hand.

'They left me with Gramps and Grandma when my sister, Laura, became ill.' Now that the floodgates were wide open, nothing was going to stop her from finishing.

'What was the matter with her?' His voice was soft now, but Jenna didn't care.

'Anorexia. She was eight years older than me, and it took her three years to die. All that time I spent with Gramps and Grandma, I hoped that Laura would get better and that I could go back home. But when she died of a heart attack, my parents didn't want me back home, they went to France. Said they couldn't bear the memories.'

'They left you behind?' He reached out to her and Jenna jerked away.

'They said they'd come back. Then they said I could go out there for a holiday. But they lied. I didn't see them again until I was eighteen, and by that time I'd made Gramps and Grandma my legal next of kin and taken their name.'

'Jen, I'm so sorry...'

'So am I, Adam. But we made a bargain that we wouldn't carry this on after you left, so don't start bending the rules on me now for your own convenience.'

She'd wounded him, even though he tried not to show it.

Her eyes filled with tears again at the thought of it. Jenna knew she was being unfair. She couldn't demand commitment from him after just one night. But she couldn't give him what he asked either.

If he'd been willing to take her with him to South America, demonstrate that there was some chance he could share his life with her, then maybe. Just maybe. But two weeks on the beach and then another parting. No. Not even if he asked her to stay. He would always be leaving, always be going away to work.

She tried to summon a smile, but couldn't. 'I should go. I'm sorry, Adam, but I think that's best.'

'Yeah. You're right, Jen. However much I wish you weren't.'

Sadness hit her, hard, right in the middle of the chest. But it was too late to repair the damage. About fifteen years too late. Jenna got to her feet and walked away from him, without looking back.

She'd shut herself in her flat and tried to concentrate on something else. Washing up. Checking her emails. Crying over Adam wasn't on her list of things to do, even if it did seem to be about the only thing that was getting done at the moment. It was only when thunder rumbled in the sky that she remembered her sketch pad, still lying under the tree in the garden where she'd left it, and ran down the fire-escape steps to fetch it.

The pad lay on the steps, about halfway up. Just about at the limit of Adam's reach from the patio, she reckoned. It was covered in plastic to protect it from the rain, and on top of it was a yellow rose. Unwilling to leave the rose where it lay, she picked it up and ran back to her flat.

Yellow. Friendship. He'd obviously been out to get it. There were no yellow roses in the garden and this one had a long stem and was perfectly shaped. She brushed the petals against her face, catching the scent of it.

They'd meant to spend the night together, but had ended up making love. And in the aftermath of that earth-turning explosion of emotion Jenna had found that, after all, there was one thing that Adam feared. One by one she picked the petals from the rose, letting them fall onto the kitchen countertop, tears running down her cheeks as she did so. When the stem was bare she dropped it into the bin, scooping the petals after it, to clean up the mess she'd made.

CHAPTER EIGHT

THE last six days had seemed like six months. Jenna had been unable to avoid bumping into Adam and they had both been polite, restrained. And she'd gone over every word that had passed between them, analysed each look, in an agony of self-reproach. Her anger had drained away, and with it some of the shadows from the past. But it was too late. Living for today was a hollow aspiration when Adam was now a part of yesterday.

She had hesitated before paging Adam, but only for a moment. This was work, and her reluctance to see him was of secondary importance. When he strode through the doors to the A and E department, he brought reinforcements in the shape of four white-coated youngsters, who were obviously students. He gave Brenda a cheery wave and made straight for Jenna, his face suddenly solemn.

'What can I do for you?'

'I've a patient who came in with a minor cut, incurred in a fall. I've cleaned and glued it.' The students were hanging on her every word and one seemed to be taking notes.

'With you so far.' Adam spoke for the whole group. His tone was professional, verging on the friendly, but that was about all. His eyes were just as blank as they'd been all week.

'Then I got the "Oh, and by the way...".' Jenna was beginning to feel uncomfortable under the four earnest stares. 'Sometimes people present with very minor things. When you've dealt with that they tell you what they've really come for.'

One of the students nodded condescendingly. 'Door-knob syndrome.'

Jenna focussed on the student's name badge. 'Gaining a patient's trust is half the battle, Mark. It's not easy to talk about some issues.'

Adam nodded, addressing the students. 'People walk out of those doors every day, having decided that they can't talk about what's really worrying them. If we let them do that, then the next time we see them it's often a real emergency.' He turned back to Jenna. 'So what's the problem?'

She proffered her notes to Adam. 'He showed me an area on his arm where his skin has lost its pigmentation. I think he may have Hansen's disease. He told me he comes from Brazil and he's over here studying. He's only been here a couple of months and he has no family in this country.'

'That's leprosy, isn't it?' There was a little rustle of unease and Mark spoke up again.

Adam ignored him. 'Can anyone tell me about Hansen's? Yes, Geeta.'

One of the other students began to reel off a list of the indications of Hansen's disease and Adam nodded her through them. 'It's one of the least communicable infectious diseases there is. Transmission is via respiratory droplets, and casual contact doesn't lead to infection. You have to be resident in an endemic area for several years before the risk of infection becomes appreciable.' Geeta stopped, gulping in a breath, and then continued.

'In Brazil it's referred to as Hansen's disease, because of the stigma surrounding the name leprosy...'

'Very nicely put. Thanks, Geeta.' Adam cut Geeta short, grinning apologetically as he did so, and flipped through the notes in his hand. 'Where is the patient?'

'Examination room two.'

'Shouldn't he be in isolation? The law says...' Mark piped up, and received a nudge in the ribs for his pains from one of his companions.

'The law says we *may* put a Hansen's patient into isolation. It's important that he has treatment now, not just for his own sake but to stop the spread of the disease, but that's an issue that hasn't arisen yet and may well not.' He flipped a glance towards Jenna, fixing his gaze back on to the students quickly. 'Dr Weston's approach, which I advise you all to note very carefully, is holistic. Treat the person, not just the disease.'

'Within the bounds of practicality.' His praise tasted bitter when there was no accompanying warmth in his eyes. 'In A and E that's something you can rarely achieve.'

'But something a good doctor, such as yourself, achieves naturally.'

Jenna cut in before Adam could say any more. 'I think that all six of us in the room might upset the patient.' Perhaps Adam and just one of the students would be appropriate, while she waited outside with the others.

Adam nodded, addressing the group. 'I agree, and it's about time I let you all go, anyway. Dr Weston and I will see the patient, and I'll update you on his progress and treatment tomorrow.' His lips twitched into what might have been a grin if he hadn't stifled it almost immediately, and Jenna tried to ignore the sweet, tingling sensation at the back of her neck. 'Emotionally and physically.'

Did he really need to put it quite like that? Perhaps he

did. On anyone else's lips, the words would have been just words. Jenna nodded politely in the students' direction and turned, walking slowly towards the examination room.

'Do you have to?'

'Do I have to what?' His guard dropped for a moment and he was all innocence. Kissable innocence, damn him. She'd hoped she might have got over that by now.

'You know. Embarrass me in front of everyone?'

'I was making a point. Mark might be bright but his bedside manner leaves a great deal to be desired.' He twisted his lips into a brief, wry smile. 'But if you don't like being complimented, I won't do it again.'

She narrowed her eyes at him. Much as she wanted to kick him, it had better wait until after he'd examined the patient she'd called him down to see.

'I guess we'll be talking about this later, then.' Adam bent to whisper the words in her ear and before she had a chance to respond he'd opened the door to examination room two, motioning her inside.

'Hector, I'm sorry to keep you waiting.' Jenna summoned a smile for the young man propped up on the bed, and got a brief one in return. 'This is Adam Sinclair, the doctor I told you about.'

Hector nodded at Adam, suspicion flashing in his dark eyes. Adam approached the bed and held out his hand. 'I imagine your English is better than my Portuguese.'

The ghost of a smile crossed Hector's face as he took Adam's hand and shook it. 'I went to an English-speaking school.'

'English it is, then. How long have you been in London?'

'One month. I start studying here in September.'

'Great. What are you studying?'

'Mathematics. I will study for three years.'

Adam grinned at him with that easy warmth that Jenna no longer had any right to. 'Rather you than me. I've no head for figures. Where are you from?'

'Manaus.'

'Ah, I know it well. I worked there for a while.' Adam leaned forward and picked up Hector's arm, examining it carefully. 'How long have you had this?'

'A little while.'

'And what about this bump under your eye? Did you do that when you fell today?'

'No.' Hector was still tense, defensive even, and Jenna couldn't fathom why. He'd got over the hard part of actually asking for help. Most people loosened up a bit after that.

'All right.' Adam's voice was soothing. 'I can take a tissue sample to find out what this is, and then I can give you the proper treatment.'

'You cannot give me the medicine now?'

Adam regarded him steadily. 'Not until I have a confirmed diagnosis.'

'If you have worked in Manaus you know what this is.'

'I can't rule Hansen's disease out. But we have to be sure. You know, don't you, that if that's what it turns out to be, then it's in its early stages and we can treat it.'

Hector nodded. 'You get the drugs and you are cured.'

'Yeah, well, just getting the drugs doesn't work. You need to actually take them. And you'll take them here, under supervision, in the hospital.'

'I can take them by myself. I do not need anyone to watch me.'

Adam regarded him thoughtfully. 'I have friends in Manaus. Good people who run a clinic there. If you are worried about someone at home, then I can put you in touch with them. They will help.'

Hector stared at him, insolence creeping into his expression.

'The drugs are free, you know that.' Adam was clearly not about to give up.

Silence.

'Okay, Hector. Who is it? A member of your family?' Adam waited and received a blank look. 'A friend? A girlfriend, maybe?'

Hector's olive skin reddened slightly. 'My family must not know.'

'That's okay, I'm not going to tell them. Neither will my colleague.' Adam gestured towards Jenna and she shook her head emphatically.

'Your friends. They will report her, though.'

Adam nodded. 'That's the law. But no harm will come to her and they can help her.'

'You do not understand.' Hector's chin jutted resolutely. He'd obviously said about as much as he was prepared to say at the moment.

'No, I don't. That's because you're not giving me all of the facts, Hector. Do you want to help your girlfriend or not? Because I'm guessing that if you don't then no one else will.'

He was putting a lot of pressure on the youth, but Jenna didn't stop him. Unless someone got to the bottom of this, a young woman might go without the treatment she desperately needed.

'You don't want to help her?' Adam made a gesture of frustration with his hand that was two inches too expansive to be British in origin. 'Who can she turn to, then?'

Hector broke. He'd put up a good fight, but Adam was too much for him, too determined. 'Her father has it. He will not tell anyone. If I send her the drugs, then she will not get sick.'

'That's not how it works, Hector. Now, listen to me. It's by no means certain or even likely that your girlfriend is infected, however much she's exposed to it. She should get checked over, though, just in case. And her father needs treatment, too.'

'He will never agree. He made her swear that she wouldn't tell anyone. She made me swear.'

'If your girlfriend's being put at risk, don't you think it's your duty to do something about it?' There was a merest hint of a flicker at the side of Adam's eye. Nothing more. 'What's her name?'

'Maria. My parents don't know about her, her family does not have money.'

'So you saw her on the quiet, eh?' Adam was grinning conspiratorially.

'Yes. My parents thought I was studying.' It seemed that now the floodgates had opened, they were well and truly open.

Adam chuckled quietly. 'Pretty name. Is she pretty?'

'Of course.'

'Does she have any symptoms?'

Hector shook his head. 'I do not think so.'

'Well, that's a good start.' Adam folded his arms across his chest. 'Okay, here's the deal, Hector. You stay here and we'll find out what's the matter with you and treat it. Meanwhile, I'll have a word with my friends. See if we can't work something out for Maria.'

'Her father will beat her if he finds out.'

'He's not going to. My friends know how to be discreet, they've done this before. And they can and will make sure that Maria's okay. They'll deal with both her medical needs and the situation with her father. That's what you want, isn't it?'

Hector nodded.

'Good.' Adam's tone was affable but brooked no argument. 'I'm bound by law to notify a case of Hansen's disease to the authorities. That means you not only have my protection, you also have that of the law, too. We'll get the skin samples done, and get you a bed here in the hospital. Once you're settled, I'll come and see you and we can talk about Maria. Is that okay?'

'Yes.' Hector's dark, liquid eyes were fixed on Adam. 'Thank you.'

'All part of the service.' Adam got to his feet. 'I can hear the trolley outside and I for one would kill for a cup of tea. What do you say I go and get some for us both?'

'He's got guts.' Adam had chatted to Hector while Jenna collected the tissue samples, and when she left the cubicle he followed her.

'You think it is Hansen's?'

'I'd be surprised if it wasn't. And he comes from Northern Brazil, where Hansen's is endemic.' He sighed. 'Even though it's greatly feared, he was willing to send the drugs that he needed to his girlfriend.'

'You can help her, can't you? Please tell me you can.' Jenna was almost pleading with him. Hector had been too proud, but she didn't care. Thirty minutes ago she might have, but that had been before Adam had crushed all her defences by going out on a limb to help the young couple.

'I've got a few influential friends who owe me a favour and if the situation's too much for the clinic to handle, they'll pull some strings.' He shrugged. 'It's not the first time I've seen this kind of situation.'

'Thank you.' Words didn't seem to cover it. The slight movement of his hand, gravitating towards her arm, told Jenna that he too felt something.

'Not going to be a problem.' He looked up and his gaze

fell on two figures sitting in the corner of the waiting room. 'What are they doing here?'

Mark and Geeta were in deep conversation together, and when Mark saw Adam he sprang to his feet.

'You'd better go and see. It looks as if it's you they're after.'

Adam let out a sigh and walked over to the pair. A quick conversation, the transfer of a blue plastic bag from Mark to Adam and then, wonder of wonders, a smile and a handshake between the two. Adam strode back towards Jenna, a look of bemused disbelief on his face.

'What's that?' Jenna pointed at the bag.

Adam opened it and peered in. 'They've been on a scavenger hunt. Bits and pieces, some soap, something to read.' He moved the newspaper to one side. 'Pen and paper, chocolate and a couple of oranges.' He looked up at Jenna, his face shining as if he had just witnessed a miracle. 'They listened when you said that Hector didn't have anyone, and went and found some things for him for his first night in the hospital.'

'That's nice of them.' Jenna looked up, and caught Mark's eye, giving him a thumbs-up and a broad smile.

Adam was shaking his head slowly. 'I was wrong about him.' Clearly nothing gave him greater pleasure than to admit it.

'Everyone has the ability to change. I believe that in my heart. If I didn't I couldn't do this job.'

'And we all have the choice.'

'Yes. I see a lot of bad things down here. Knives, acid, drink and drugs, all kinds of violence. I see some good things, too.' She indicated the carrier bag. 'Random acts of kindness.'

He leaned in, just close enough for their conversation to be private, not too close that anyone would remark on it. 'You have the capacity to see what people might be, not what they are. It's a great gift.'

Much good it did her. She saw what Adam could be and how much he'd changed already. An exceptional doctor, skilled, professional and caring, who had somehow reclaimed his passion in the last few weeks, lifting his already considerable gifts to a whole new level. But that did nothing to close the deep crevasse that lay between the two of them. Jenna bit her lip and studied the floor.

'I have to go and give these things to Hector.' He indicated the carrier bag that he was holding. 'Mark and Geeta are hanging around. I said I'd ask if he wanted them to go up to the ward with him. It'd be good for him to have someone of his own age. He needs a friend.'

'Yes. That's a nice idea.' She reached out and touched his arm. It was okay. She knew the score and that was okay.

'Thanks.' His face softened and she saw the man who had haunted her dreams for the last six nights. 'Thanks, Jen.'

CHAPTER NINE

THE dream was different this time. Normally Adam was not aware of having dreamt, only of the terror of waking and the dull horror that followed. But this time the dream seemed to go on for an eternity.

Someone was screaming. His own roar sounded from somewhere in the distance and when he looked at his hands there was blood. The butt of a gun and an arm. Light and shadow. No, not light and shadow, it was patchy, half-pigmented skin. The sun in his eyes then on his back as he tried to crawl to Elena.

He tried to push himself into wakefulness, but the dream held him tight, replaying the disjointed images again and again, like a loop of badly damaged film. Finally, with a cry that seemed to resound through his dreams and into the waking world, he managed to wrench his eyes open.

'Adam.' He was lying on his back, sweat soaking into the sheet beneath him, fighting for breath, and all he could think about was Jenna's voice. This had to stop.

'Adam. It's okay, you've been dreaming. But you're back.'

He jerked himself upright. She was perched on a large linen chest that stood in the corner of the room, deep in shadow. 'Jenna. What the hell…? How long have you been here?'

'Ten minutes. A little longer maybe.'

'How did you get in?' He looked over to the French doors, which he had fastened securely before he had gone to bed but which were now wide open.

'I have a key, remember? I heard you moaning, and when you started yelling I came down and banged on the door to wake you up. When you didn't, I went and fetched the key.'

Why would she do that? The thought of her watching him while he battled his most shameful secret filled Adam with self-loathing. A little bit of it spilled out in her direction and he felt his lip curl. 'You wanted to see, did you?'

'No, not particularly. But I did want to hear.' Her voice was carefully measured, as if she was making an effort not to rise to his bait. 'Take this.' She rose and walked over to the bed, holding out a piece of paper. She was wearing a white cotton nightdress under the silky robe that he liked so much, and Adam noticed that her hand was trembling. 'You were speaking in Spanish. I've written it down, but I don't know what it means.'

He didn't take the paper and she put it down on the nightstand. 'You should look at it now, while the dream's still fresh. Perhaps it'll help.'

She was leaving him alone to read what she had written, not even asking for thanks, although her quiet courage deserved far more than that. 'Wait.'

She froze. The word hung in the air between them and Adam wished he could grab it back. He should have just let her go. She didn't need to see this. He didn't want to show her.

'What is it?' Jenna moved slowly back to the bed, sitting down on the edge of it.

'I...' He couldn't say it. He wanted her to stay, but couldn't get past the clamour in his head, pulling him back down into the dream and its terrors.

'Would you like me to stay?'

She'd said it for him, and suddenly that was all he wanted. Damn the dreams. Damn the terrors. She could cut through them, with one touch of her fingers. 'Yes. If that's not too much to ask of you.' He picked the paper up from the nightstand and handed it to her.

Her smile, as she slipped the paper into her pocket, made the task ahead of them seem bearable. 'Of course not. Why don't I make some tea and we can find out what's on there together?'

Adam pulled on his jeans and a sweatshirt, then went through to the sitting room and switched on a lamp. She appeared from the kitchen, two steaming mugs in her hands, each with the tag from a herbal tea company draped over the side. In her bright, flowing robe, with her hair tumbling loose around her shoulders, she looked like some ethereal pre-Raphaelite beauty.

She put the cups on the coffee table with a clatter and plonked herself down next to him on the sofa, producing the paper from her pocket. 'Let's see, then, shall we? I'm afraid it's not that much. I wrote it down phonetically because I didn't understand what you were saying. I did think of recording you on my phone, but...' she shrugged '...I couldn't do that.'

He was grateful for that. It was going to be difficult enough to hear what she'd written down on that paper and Adam was not sure that he could listen to his own disjointed ravings. She'd taken that burden and kept it for herself.

'Thank you, Jen.' He tried to emphasise the words so that they might contain some measure of the gratitude he felt, and craned over her shoulder to look at the paper. She'd been writing in the dark, and some of the lines of text veered off course, overlapping each other, but they were clear enough. He concentrated on the words, trying to sound them in his head but the noise was back, taking away his ability to concentrate.

'Perhaps it would be easier if I read it aloud.' She ran her finger along the first line, reading slowly and carefully.

'*Espera* means wait.'

'Right.' She paused. 'You mean it makes sense?'

'I know what it means. I've no idea why I said it.' Somewhere at the back of his mind there seemed to be an echo of something, but when he reached for it, it disappeared.

'What does it mean?'

'Wait, wait, wait. There's no need for that.'

She searched his face. 'And you don't remember saying anything like that? Or who you might have said it to?'

'No. Is there anything else?'

'You shouted the word *sangre* quite a few times. Does that mean blood?'

Adam nodded. That didn't get them any further either. He already knew that there had been blood. 'Yes. That's good, though. It's something.' He tried to sound convincing.

'Okay, well, what about this? *Detras de mi.*' She studied the paper carefully. 'I'm not sure whether that's with an *i* or an *e*.'

'It's *mi,* with an i. It means me. Get behind me.' A small glimmer of hope ignited in his brain. Perhaps, after all, he'd tried to protect Elena. But it was only hope. No recognition, no memories. Nothing but wishful thinking.

She'd reached for a pad that was lying on the coffee

table and torn a sheet from it. 'Here. Write it all down, before we forget.' She handed him a pen and Adam obediently wrote down the phrases, in Spanish and English. 'Now, what about this?' She ran her finger across her sheet again, silently mouthing the sounds.

Adam craned over, following her finger. 'Don't bother with that. I'm…er…making my feelings very plain at this point.'

'Oh.' Her finger stopped suddenly. 'Good for you. I hope you gave them what for.' She tapped the paper in front of him. 'Write that down as well.'

'But it doesn't mean anything.'

'No, but it's what you said. It might jog your memory later on.'

She had a point. Adam wrote the words down, omitting the English version. There wasn't an exact translation anyway. 'Is that everything?'

'Pretty much.' She surveyed the sheet in front of him. 'You shouted *lepra* a couple of times, but I guess you were just getting mixed up in your dream. Seeing Hector the other day at work.'

Adam put his head in his hands, straining to remember. There was something, right on the edge of his consciousness, that he just couldn't reach. 'I guess so. I don't know, Jen.'

'Okay. Okay, relax. Stop trying.' Her hands were on his wrists, pulling them away from his face. 'Just take deep breaths and try and clear your mind. I'll be back in one minute.' She sprang to her feet, almost running from the room, and Adam heard her climbing the steps outside, up to her own balcony. She was back almost immediately, carrying one of the large artist's pads that she used for sketching.

'Let's try this.' She put the pad down in front of him

and took his hands, putting them palm down onto a clean page. 'Now spread your fingers…that's right. Feel the texture.' The thick paper felt silky smooth under his touch.

'This isn't going to work, Jen.'

'Maybe not. You've tried pretty much everything else.'

'In other words, just shut up and get on with it.'

'Exactly. Can you feel the paper?'

Adam closed his eyes. 'Yeah. I feel it.'

'Okay, now just let your mind drift. Let the paper take on a shape, any shape. Don't try to control it, just let it happen.'

Adam wasn't buying this. But she'd stuck with him this far and he appreciated that. He took a deep breath, feeling his shoulders loosen as he exhaled. The paper was cool, textured under his fingers. He did as Jenna told him, concentrating on its feel under each one of his fingers in turn. Then he waited. For what seemed like an eternity.

Suddenly an image shot into his head. 'A gun butt. No…a rifle.' He could feel beads of cold sweat forming on his brow.

'Good. That's fine. What else?' He could feel her hands on his shoulders, keeping him from harm.

'Someone's arm… Light and shade… *La lepra.*' He almost whispered the words.

'Are you sure?'

'Positive.' Adam's eyes snapped open. He could see the arm in his mind's eye now, clear and detailed. The skin wasn't that of a young man. It was an older man, gnarled and twisted with disease. 'It's not Hector, it's someone else. I've got it now. I can see it.'

'Good, that's great.' Her face was shining with success.

Adam looked down at the sheet in front of him, the outline of his hands still faintly visible from where the absorbent paper had soaked up the sweat from his fingers. 'I felt it, Jen.'

She shrugged. 'You were drawing it in your mind's eye. My grandfather taught me how to draw and he showed me how to do it. Putting your hands on the paper seems to help.' She focussed on the pad. 'It's not actually there. Obviously.'

'But it works.' The image was clear in his head now.

'Well, not for me. I think it's a load of hocus pocus, but Gramps swore by it.' She grinned at him, wayward and entirely entrancing. 'I expect it's just the relaxing thing, thinking about something else.' She ripped the top sheet off the pad, exposing a fresh leaf. 'Now, tell me what this hand you remember looked like.'

It took them an hour, Adam carefully describing the remembered images and Jenna transcribing them on to paper. When they'd finished he was exhausted. She laid the sheets of drawing paper and his written page on the coffee table in front of them. 'It's not enough, is it?'

He put his hand over hers, trying to give the consolation that he didn't feel. 'But it's a start, eh? It shows that the memories are there, at least some of them.'

'If only...' Her voice was laden with disappointment. She had to see the ambiguity of the disjointed phrases. Had his rapid invective been after Elena had been shot or had he argued with the bandits and prompted her shooting? *Get behind me*—the words of a hero trying to protect someone or the words of a coward as he ran away?

'It's a start.' He squeezed her hand. 'Thank you.' There was nothing more to do now but to go back to bed and try and get some sleep. And if he craved a few more minutes of her company before that happened, he knew that it was pointless. He would always want more time with her, however much he took.

'Do you need me to stay?'

'No.' He didn't want Jenna to see any more of this than she already had. 'But can I take you out for breakfast in the morning?'

'I'd like that.' She sprang to her feet and Adam followed her into the bedroom. Head high, and without so much as a glance at the rumpled sheets on the bed, she slipped through the billowing muslin curtains. Then, closing the French doors behind her, she was gone, like a wraith in the night.

Jenna had woken early, and had not been able to turn over in bed and sleep again. Instead she'd showered and dressed, wondering whether Adam was going to make good on his promise. Maybe she'd just pop downstairs, see if he was awake.

She crept gingerly down the fire-escape steps and peered through the window. His bedroom was empty, the duvet and pillows straightened and neat. He must be up, but she could hardly tap on his bedroom door now that daylight was flooding through the windows.

Tiptoeing back up the steps, she walked through her flat and out of the front door. If she was going to go downstairs, she'd use the proper route. Halfway down, she caught sight of him, leaning in the open doorway to his flat, arms folded and a smile on his face.

'You're up.' Jenna tried to sound surprised.

'Yep. And I'm starving. Are you ready for breakfast?'

He'd remembered. And he was waiting for her. The bone-wrenching sadness of the last week dissolved, like a morning mist under the heat of the sun. 'Ready when you are.'

He didn't reply but pulled the door closed behind him with a smile. She wanted to run to him, but she didn't.

Instead she took his arm when he offered it, hanging on tight.

Adam didn't mention last night's dream as they strolled to the small café on the high road and Jenna let the matter lie. If he wanted to talk about it, he would, and there was no sense in pushing it. Finding an empty table, they ordered coffee and two full English breakfasts. Jenna was hungry too. Perhaps not for food, but she felt hungry for life again, and a good breakfast seemed the place to start.

'So it was your grandfather who taught you to draw?' Adam was tackling his breakfast with verve.

'Yes. He was a painter.'

'Really?' Adam's fork was suddenly still, poised between his plate and his mouth. 'Do you have any of his paintings in your flat?'

He knew as well as she did that she didn't. It wasn't that she didn't love them, but Gramps's paintings could be unsettling at times. A little too much truth. 'They're quite big.'

He nodded. 'That's a shame.' He waited for a moment, giving her a chance to elaborate, and then put the fork into his mouth.

'I do have some. In storage.' Suddenly Jenna wanted him to see the pictures, if only to show him that she wasn't completely alone in the world. Her grandparents had never deserted her.

'Yes?' There was a glimmer of interest in his face. More than just a glimmer.

'I have them at the house.' Jenna returned her attention to the plate in front of her. A man like Adam, who believed in one fixed version of the truth about himself, would be challenged by Gramps's view of the world, the many truths that showed so clearly in his paintings. If he did want to see them, he was going to have to ask.

'Do you ever show them to anyone?' He was nosing at

the bait and Jenna almost held her breath, waiting to see if he'd bite.

'Of course I do, I'm very proud of them.'

He bit. With a grin that told her he knew that he'd been snared. 'May I see them?'

'Yes, of course. After breakfast?'

'I'd like that.'

'Wait till you've seen them. They can be challenging.'

'More than I can take?' His gaze met hers and suddenly this wasn't about paintings anymore. It was about two people, struggling to find a way to connect without tearing each other apart.

'I wouldn't ask any more than that, Adam.'

'No. Nor I you.' He slid his hand across the table towards hers and the deal was sealed in the moment that their fingers touched.

'Friends, then?' Jenna smiled at him.

'Always.' He tapped the edge of her plate with the tip of his fork. 'And since we are friends, maybe I can enquire whether you're going to eat your bacon. Shame to let it go to waste…'

'I'm saving it for last.' Jenna coiled her arm protectively around her plate and caught the waiter's eye. 'George, will you bring some more bacon, please?'

'And toast.' Adam's lips twitched into a satisfied grin. Jenna was not sure now which one of them had snared the other. 'I assume you're saving your toast for last, too.'

'As it happens, I am.' She picked the coffee pot up and tilted it towards his cup. 'But you can have the rest of the coffee if you want it.'

He nodded, and Jenna refilled his cup. Suddenly she didn't care who'd snared who, or what the consequences might be. This happiness was far too good to waste.

* * *

Adam had been expecting a dark, cluttered loft space, much the same as his own. Instead, Jenna led him past her front door and up a set of winding stairs, unlocking a door at the top and leading him into a large attic room. Odd angles and a sloping ceiling that followed the shape of the roof. High beams and white-painted walls. Light bursting in through the large dormer windows, flooding the space.

'What do you think?' She twirled around, showing off the space. 'This used to be my grandfather's studio, and now I use it.'

He saw that. The clutter of paints and canvasses. Photographs pinned up on the walls, some old and faded and some more recent. The whole space was alive with light and colour, bearing both the stamp of the man who had created it and Jenna's lighter hand.

She was leafing through a set of canvasses, stacked and wrapped in a shaded corner for safekeeping. 'Help me with this, will you?'

He helped her slide the one she wanted out from the stack, and watched while she removed the wrappings. 'So is this a self-portrait?'

'No, he never painted himself. It's of Laura, my sister. He painted it just after she died and I sat with him and helped him.' She gave a little shrug. 'With some of the brushstrokes.'

Adam could see it all. A man helping his granddaughter come to terms with her loss through the thing that connected them both. The thought made him smile.

She stood, the canvas propped against her legs, its back towards him. 'Everything's here in this painting, Adam. You just have to choose how to see it.'

His heart seemed to beat a little faster. 'May I see it, then?'

The painting was stunning. Powerful, intimate and quite breathtaking. A young woman, painted in fine and loving detail, standing on a beach. She was blond, blue-eyed and blooming with promise. Serene, despite the rage and grief in the harsh brushstrokes of the sea, to her left. Adam stared, dumbstruck.

'Do you like it?' She was nervous, her fingers fluttering across the edges of the canvas.

'*Like* isn't the word that springs to mind. It's magnificent.' He stepped back to get a better view, and as he did so, the seemingly anarchic shapes of the waves formed into the suggestion of a gaunt face.

'You see what I mean?'

Adam stared at the painting. He saw. 'He was a brave man.' The stubborn refusal to turn away from tragedy, to face it and own it, reminded him of someone. 'Was he a redhead, too?'

She laughed. 'Not when I knew him. He was when he was younger. Grandma said she fell in love with his hot-headedness.'

Even with Jenna in the room, Adam still couldn't quite tear his eyes from the painting. 'She was very beautiful. Your grandfather painted kindness, too.'

'Yes, she was. She was one of those people who seem to be good at everything. Out of the two of us, she was the pretty one as well.' The small quirk of her lips told Adam that he had hit a sore spot.

'You think so?'

'That's what everyone used to say.'

'Everyone? What did your grandfather say?' Adam took a chance and trusted the man who had painted that astonishing portrait.

She shrugged. 'Well, Gramps never did go along with what everyone else said. Artistic temperament, you know.'

'I see clear-sightedness in this painting.' A lot of things were beginning to make sense to Adam. The second-best child who'd lost her sister and been abandoned by her parents. He reckoned that was about enough hurt to make anyone diffident about accepting praise.

She stood, biting her lip for a moment, as if she was wrestling with an insoluble brain-teaser. Then she tossed it aside in frustration. 'I just wanted you to see it. That's all.'

'Thank you. I'm honoured that you shared this with me.' Her ears began to go pink, and she propped the painting against the wall, sitting on the stool by the easel.

'I'm glad you like it. It means a lot to me.'

'Did your grandfather ever paint you?'

She rubbed her palms together, uneasily. 'Yes, he did.'

'Are you going to show me?'

'It's... It's...'

'It's what? Not very good?'

She rose to the bait magnificently, tossing her head and stalking over to the stack of paintings. Adam noticed that she knew which one to select straight away, and that this one was loosely bound, as if it had often been taken out of its wrappings.

'He painted this when I was twenty. It was pretty much his last painting.'

She twisted the canvas abruptly round for him to see, and the force of it nearly knocked him off his feet. Jenna sat on a high stool, dressed in jeans and baseball boots, her hands planted on her knees in a posture of quiet assurance. A rainbow-coloured shawl hung over her right shoulder, contrasting vibrantly with her plain white shirt.

'Wow! That's...' He was unable to find the words just yet. It wasn't that this was a beautifully executed portrait of a gorgeous woman. Jenna's grandfather had somehow captured her essence, the fascinating contrast between beauty and vulnerability, practicality and her more artistic nature.

The real thing quirked her lips downwards. 'Gramps always was an old softie. He's done me a few favours.'

Adam bent to examine the portrait more carefully. Behind Jenna was the organised clutter of the attic studio, with one addition that was conspicuously absent from the room he was now in. A mirror, right behind her, the back of her head and shoulders reflected in it. Hair swept up in a complex arrangement of shining curls, even redder than the original. Bare shoulders, crossed by the dark green straps of what was obviously an evening dress.

'What's that?' The high back of the stool had something slung carelessly around the support, half-obscured by her shoulder.

She didn't reply and he looked again, and couldn't keep the grin from his face when he made it out. It was a coronet. Her grandfather had painted her as she was, but also how she seemed to him. 'An ordinary woman, who's also a princess.'

Jenna nodded. 'It's one of his little jokes. He used to call me princess sometimes.'

'It's beautiful.' Adam peered at the bottom right-hand side of the picture, wondering if his suspicions were right. There was a small signature there. 'Your grandfather was Alex Weston?' The man who'd painted many beautiful women in the 1960s and 1970s, then disappeared from the limelight to paint the ordinary, lending everyday things a little magic with his brush.

'Yes. Are you impressed?'

'Not by the name. But the kind of man who can paint something with so much love in it must have been quite extraordinary.'

He could see from her eyes that he'd given the right answer. The one she wanted to hear from him. 'That's a nice thing to say.' She grinned. 'I don't talk about Gramps's painting all that much because people get all excited about him being famous.'

'And that's not the most important thing about him.'

'No. Not by a long chalk.' The approval in her eyes told Adam that he'd passed some sort of test.

'Jenna, will you do something?'

'What's that?'

'Will you bring this painting downstairs? Put it in your sitting room somewhere so that you can look at it. Listen to your grandfather when he tells you what he thinks of you.'

She looked at him as if there was some catch to what he was saying. 'I'll think about it.'

'Do that. It's a beautiful painting and shouldn't be hidden away up here. Even if it does have one flaw.'

'What?' She twisted round to examine the painting, ready to spring to her grandfather's defence.

'I'm banking on your grandfather having been the first to say it. It doesn't do you justice.'

The flare in her eyes told Adam that he was right. She'd obviously just about reached the limit of what she was willing to admit to, though.

'Don't you try and wheedle your way around me with compliments.'

'I'm not. Not just yet, anyway.' She'd leant the painting against the wall, next to the one of Laura, and Adam caught her arm, spinning her round and imprisoning her in a loose embrace. Seized by a sudden awkwardness, he propelled her out of the door and closed it firmly behind them.

'Not while Gramps is watching, eh?' She was grinning up at him, snuggling close.

'Some things he doesn't need to see.' Adam ran his fingers over the filmy material of her collar. Soft, like an inferior copy of her skin.

'I doubt he'd mind.'

'Minding and seeing are two different things. Are you coming downstairs with me, or do I have to throw you over my shoulder?' She caught her breath in delighted shock at the abruptness of his demand and he silenced her with a kiss. Enough with words. He'd show her how beautiful she was if it killed him. And if the last time he'd had her in his bed was anything to go by, it might just do that.

CHAPTER TEN

JENNA had made her decision. And in the five days since she and Adam had been back together, she'd not regretted it once. Colleague, lover, friend—he did all of them better than anyone she'd ever known before. But now the time they had left was dwindling fast. Five days, not counting today. Saturday, Sunday, Monday, Tuesday, Wednesday. Actually, only half of Wednesday, because he had an evening flight and Jenna had already decided not to go to the airport with him. Airports made her cry.

Adam was officially not working today, but Jenna knew that he was in the hospital somewhere. Finishing off. Saying goodbye. He had already sent her a text to meet him in the canteen at lunchtime, and today she told Brenda that she would be taking her full hour's break. A and E wasn't busy, and just the once wouldn't hurt.

He wasn't alone. Two blond heads, sitting opposite him at the table, and next to him an older man, Julie's father, who jumped to his feet when he saw Jenna, motioning her to sit next to Adam, while he shifted across to sit with his daughters.

'Ah, thank goodness.' Adam gave her a beseeching look. 'I'm dying here and Terry's giving me no support.'

Julie's father laughed. 'I learned a long time ago that I'm no match for two teenagers once they get started.

Anyway, what's so bad about having a blog? I think it's a good idea.'

'Yeah, see,' Julie crowed, turning to Jenna. 'Emma and I will set it up for him, since he doesn't know how, and he can write all about the places he goes and the jungle and stuff. Then we'll know what he's up to.'

'Sounds like a plan.' Jenna wasn't sure what kind of plan. The thought that it might be possible to keep up with Adam's activities filled her with a mixture of dread and delight.

'See, Jenna thinks it's a good idea,' Emma chimed in. 'We can give it a name, can't we, Jules?'

'Yeah. Dr Danger Defies… Defies what, Em?'

Emma's brow creased in thought. 'Dunno. Dr Danger Defies Deadly something.'

'Ducks.' Jenna giggled and Adam's head sank into his hands.

There was a chorus of 'No's' from around the table and she feigned surprise.

'Ducks can be quite vicious at times.'

'You don't get ducks in the jungle.' Julie admonished her.

'You don't get broadband in the jungle either.' Adam was putting up a creditable fight.

Julie rolled her eyes. 'Well, you write it down in a notebook and take some pictures and then update your blog later. They must have broadband somewhere in South America.'

'Yeah. Quite a lot of places actually. But I'm not having you call it Dr Danger does anything. If I'm going to write a blog, it'll be under my own name. That's final.'

Julie and Emma exchanged glances. Jenna recognised that trick. Suggest something outrageous and then accept a compromise. Which was generally the thing you wanted in the first place.

'Okay.' Julie couldn't keep the smirk out of her voice. 'Not a bad tag line, though. Dr Danger Does Anything.'

'No. Adam Sinclair. It's that or nothing.' Adam seemed to have reached his sticking point. 'And don't expect me to update it more than once a week.'

'That's okay. We don't have time to comment more than once a week.' Emma was grinning, too. 'Anyway, Julie can't type at the moment, so I'll have to do it for both of us.'

'No way.' Adam turned to Julie. 'I know your fingers are stiff, but the burn therapist told you to keep them moving gently, didn't she? You can type just a couple of words, slowly, to let me know how you're doing.'

Busted. He'd just given himself away, to Jenna if not to Julie and Emma. He'd been playing them at their own game. Giving them something to do together, keeping in touch with them. Letting them both know that he wanted to hear how they were doing. She shot Adam a grin. 'Yes. I'll look in as well and put some comments on, so I'd better see yours there as well, Julie. And Emma's.'

'You will.' Julie's voice had a note of confidence in it. She was so different now from the pain-racked, terrified teenager that Jenna had seen a month ago in A and E. So much care, from so many people, and this was what could be achieved. 'I might even do a blog of my own.'

They'd said their goodbyes. Terry had shaken Adam's hand as if he could work it loose from his arm and take it home with him as a memento, and had given Jenna a hug and a kiss. Jenna had hugged Julie and Emma, promising to see them both soon, and Adam had kissed each of them on the cheek.

'Are you crying?' He sat back down and offered her a paper napkin.

'No.'

'Right. I wouldn't have blamed you if you were. Seeing them both like this. You usually see the start of the process, not the end.'

She'd been thinking about that. How she so seldom got to follow through with her patients. It had been such a pleasure to see Julie and Emma today, maybe not quite whole again, but well on the road to it. 'Do you think they'll be okay, Adam?'

He blew out a breath. 'Difficult to say. They've got exams, boys, careers, marriages, children, the property market and social networking to contend with. Bit of a tall order.'

'Stop it. You know what I mean.'

'Yeah, they'll be okay. Julie's got the best medical care, they've got good family support and counselling help.'

'Yes, I heard you'd pushed the counselling through. And Terry told me about your offer, too. That was good of you.'

Adam shrugged as if it was nothing. 'It may not come to that. Julie might not need any follow-up surgery, and if she does, she might not need me to do it. But she can always come to me, even if she just needs someone to talk to.'

'That's the most important thing right now. That she knows she has someone she trusts, who'll be there if she needs it. It's giving her the confidence to look forward to the future now.'

'Yeah. Hope so.' His lips twisted and for a moment he seemed to feel what Jenna was feeling. About his future and hers. Then the moment was gone, and he grinned.

'So what do you think of my foray into the world of cyberspace, then?'

'I think you're a manipulative, two-timing rat.'

The grin broadened. 'Well, thank you, you do say the nicest things. I've been thinking of doing a blog for ages.' He leaned across the table towards her. 'So are you going to join in then? Send me a few comments. You can be Dr Delicious. I quite like the sound of Dr Danger and Dr Delicious.'

'You'll be Dr Decapitated if you're not careful.' Jenna did too, but she'd decapitate herself rather than admit it. 'It would serve you right if I decided to send Julie and Emma a few sketches of you to put on there.'

He paled slightly. 'Which one? Not the one you did last night, Jen… Why do you always have to wait until I'm asleep, anyway?'

'Because you won't stay still for long enough when you're awake. Actually, I was thinking of the cartoons.'

'Oh, yeah, they're great.' He was grinning again. 'Just right.'

Adam wanted to make the most of these last few days they had together. He'd made his decision to go, and nothing was going to sway him from that. It might not be easy, but it was the right thing to do. Jenna needed a man who could commit, someone who would take care of her. He was unable to do either.

They were both adults, though, knew the score and had decided to take a taste of what life was ultimately going to deny them. Just a few days. And the more he could make her smile in those few days, the better.

His campaign started in earnest that evening. He'd taken her to see a film in a small independent cinema, where armchairs replaced rows of seats, and drinks were served in the auditorium before the beginning of the film. Then on to a South American restaurant, run by friends of his and home late.

'You, sweetheart, are the prettiest card sharp I've ever met.'

She laughed, dumping the bag of coins on the coffee table. Two pounds fifty-seven in pennies. 'And you are the worst I've ever met. You're so easy to read.'

'For you maybe.' Sometimes he wished that he didn't feel so transparent under her gaze. 'So what am I thinking right now?' He pulled her into his arms and kissed her, savouring the faint taste of tequila on her lips.

'You're wondering if you can distract me enough to get your hands on my bag of pennies. And the answer is that you can't.'

'Not even close. That tequila tastes nice.'

She giggled. 'It was. I've never had tequila before.'

'Well, that was the good stuff. You don't just throw it down for a buzz, you sip it slowly, like brandy. Leave the salt and lemons in the kitchen cupboard.'

She nodded. 'Pity you were driving. Was that a bottle of it I saw you put in the car?'

'Yeah. Thought I'd give it to Rob. He can crack it open when the baby's born.'

'Good idea. I might pop over there and give him a hand with that.' She twisted her lips in an expression of sudden regret, and it was Adam's turn to know what she was thinking. Unless the baby came in the next four days, he wouldn't be there. He hated it too, but there was no point in dwelling on it.

'So, now that you've cleaned me out of small change…' He grinned down at her, endeavouring to make her smile again. 'Don't suppose there's much chance of winning it back, is there?'

'Not a great deal. You could try.' She looped one finger inside his shirt, and the room swam slightly before his eyes. Those moments of anticipation, when he knew exactly where they were headed. Without breaking the kiss, he backed her through the door and down the hallway towards the bedroom.

He woke in the middle of the night. A warm haze was spreading through his body, moving from his chest to his groin and then fluttering up to his chest again. He felt as if he were being bathed in sunlight, sharp sensations of pleasure pulsing through his body, and he moved drowsily in time with them.

His eyes snapped open. Jenna had just climbed on top of him, astride his hips, her skin pale against his. He loved that. The way her skin seemed almost to shimmer in the half-light, contrasting with the darker tones of his own.

'Hey, you.'

'Mmm. Is this my wake-up call?'

'Yes.' She smiled mischievously. 'You like it?'

The answer to that one was obvious. Adam stretched languidly beneath her, settling his hands onto her hips. 'I love the view.'

She laughed quietly. She was the same woman he'd first made love with two weeks ago, but she'd changed, too. Then his compliments had been received awkwardly, as if she hadn't quite believed them. But he had kept them coming and slowly she had begun to accept them. Now she was revelling in them.

He reached over and flipped the bedside lamp on, laughing as she blinked. 'You are so beautiful. Your skin's like porcelain, did you know that?'

She grinned at him. 'What else?'

'Flame-haired.'

'Mmm. You deserve something for all these nice things you're saying about me.' She reached over to the bedside cabinet and tore at a foil packet. Lifting herself up onto her knees, she rolled the condom down in place, taking the opportunity to caress him at the same time.

'That feels…so much better when you do it, honey.' Adam was fighting for control. Battling not to sink into incoherence. He didn't want her to just know how he felt about her. He wanted her to hear it from his own lips.

Carefully, she sank back onto him, taking him inside her as she went. He felt his body begin to tremble and his hands tighten on her waist. Dipping towards him, she whispered against his cheek 'This is all for you, sweetheart.'

'Oh, really?' He canted his hips, gripping hers to control her movements, and she gasped, colour rising in her cheeks. Again, and she arched her back, throwing her head back. Magnificent. Alluring. He told her so, in as many words as he could summon. He told her that he loved the way her eyes caught the light. The way she'd been so ready for him, and that they seemed to fit together so well.

The balance tipped again, and she rocked backwards, twisting her hips as she went, and his eyes snapped upwards in their sockets, quite of their own accord. There were no words for this, none that he could think of anyway. His body shuddered beneath hers, and he gave himself over to the waves of pure sensation that ebbed and flowed along with her movements.

Finally he could stand it no more. It took just one movement and he had twisted her over onto her back. She gave a delighted squeal, and Adam realised that this was what she had wanted all along.

She saved the best for last, her body blossoming under his like living flame, her muscles tightening around him, till he couldn't hold on any longer. He thought he called her name, but he wasn't sure. Maybe it was just that it was the only thing in his head at the moment. And then he almost passed out from sheer, head-spinning, heart-grabbing pleasure.

'Jen.' Somehow he'd managed to collapse beside her, rather than right on top of her. 'Jenna, honey.'

'Mmm. So nice. You are *so* nice.' Her voice was small, choked with emotion, and he pulled her into the curve of his body, holding her tight until she began to drift off to sleep in his arms.

When she woke, light was filtering through the curtains. Jenna lay on her back in his arms, staring at the ceiling, wondering whether it would be considered kidnap to lock him in here all weekend.

Mind you, perhaps he'd be the one to lock *her* in. Or perhaps they'd just have done with any dispute in the matter and lock each other in. She shifted a little so she could see his face. Long lashes, closed over those beautiful eyes, a slight smile curving his lips, as if his dreams were good ones.

A noise from the sitting room caught her attention and his eyes fluttered open. 'It's only my phone.' Jenna didn't move. 'Whoever it is can leave a message.'

'No, they can't. I want you all to myself today.'

'Oh, do you?' She loved the early mornings. Lying next to him, talking lazily. 'Oh, who on earth is it?' The sound of her mobile drifted through from the hallway.

He rolled away from her. 'Better get it. It might be urgent.'

'Well, it can wait.' She lay on her back, arms folded.

'You'll only be wondering if you don't find out who it is.'

He was right. She climbed out of bed and padded through to the hallway, just in time to hear her mobile stop ringing. One missed call.

'Who was it?'

'Rob. What does he want at this hour?' Jenna sat back down on the bed. 'Suppose I'd better call back, just in case it's anything. Cassie's very close to her due date now.'

Before she could dial, Adam's phone started to ring and he grabbed it from the bedside table. 'It's okay, he's calling me now.' He punched the Answer key and spoke into the phone. 'What is it, mate? It's seven o'clock in the morning.'

She could hear Rob's voice on the other end of the line, talking fast. Suddenly Adam sat up. 'Okay... Sure, text me the address. Jenna? I imagine she's in bed at this time in the morning and didn't answer her phone... No, don't worry, I can track her down.'

'What is it?'

Adam ran his hand through his hair. 'There's a demolition site, just around the corner?'

'Yes, I know it.'

'Apparently someone got in there overnight. There's been a collapse and there are casualties. The fire department is digging them out now, and it would help if there was a doctor on the scene, but the shift in A and E already have their hands full.'

There was no question that he was going to go. Or that she'd go, too. He was into his jeans in a moment, picking up the rest of his clothes and heading for the front door. 'I'll just go and get changed. If you've got a heavy jacket and boots, put them on. It's going to be rough work down there.'

They went on foot, Jenna taking him at a run along a back alley that led almost directly to the scene. A police cordon was already blocking the road, and she flashed her hospital tags at the constable who was standing by the fluttering strip of yellow and black plastic stretched across the road.

'Doctors. Let us through.'

The young constable looked relieved, then shot a glance up the road. 'Where's the ambulance?'

'It probably won't be here for a few minutes. I live just around the corner. Will you direct the ambulance crew through to us as soon as they arrive?'

'Right you are.' The constable lifted the tape, and Adam ducked under it, motioning her through.

He was ahead of her, jogging down the road to where a fire engine was parked outside a wooden hoarding, which sheltered the site from view. Adam made for what looked like the senior man there and was already talking rapidly to him when Jenna caught up.

'Parker, Fire and Rescue. I've called for backup, but the whole building's unstable and we can't use any heavy lifting gear. My men are having to move the rubble by hand. Any sign of the ambulance yet?'

'Not yet. How many in there?'

'Three, we think. Can't tell just yet.'

Another man, florid and rotund, who looked as if he had just rolled out of bed, marched up to them. 'This is my site. What the hell's going on?'

Parker rounded on him. 'No, it's *my* site now. Stay back there, where I told you.' He turned back to Adam. 'No point going in there just yet. It's just more weight and the floor's already unstable. My men will let you know when they've reached the casualties.'

'These two can't go in.' The florid man spoke up again. 'Listen, I'm the site manager, and my insurance doesn't cover this. It's one thing for the fire department to go tramping in there, but health and safety regulations state quite clearly—'

'We're doctors. We can help your men.' Jenna spoke calmly, trying to defuse the situation.

'I don't care if you're bloody Mother Theresa. You as much as cut your finger in there and I'm liable.' The man was waving his arm, practically shouting in her face.

'You heard what the lady said.' Adam's voice was as cold as steel. Ten times more threatening, and the site manager took a step back.

'They're not my men. Bloody scavengers, after what they could get.' The man's voice tailed off and he turned, walking away to lean against a dark blue Mercedes parked next to the fire truck. Jenna turned and caught a glimpse of Adam's face. She wasn't surprised the site manager had backed off. That glare was enough to face down a basilisk.

'What was that all about?' Adam turned off the glare and looked questioningly at Parker.

'Oh, Mr High and Mighty Site Manager was the first down here. Apparently some of the neighbours heard something going on and called the number on the hoarding. There were some men inside, looking for architectural salvage. Happens quite a lot in these old buildings, it's worth a fair bit. I wouldn't be surprised if he was in on it as there's no sign of a forced entry.'

'And he called you?' Jenna was trying to work out why the site manager had called the fire service.

'Yes. Covering his own back, afraid of any passersby being injured by anything. It was us who called for an ambulance.' Parker's face showed exactly what he thought of that. 'I'll make sure my report makes that very clear.' His eyes flipped to the end of the street. 'Ah, here they are.'

An ambulance was making its way down the road,

lights still flashing, and Parker swung into action. 'Right, I'll just go and get them up to speed. You two, find some hard hats, they're in the back of the truck. I'll take you in there but it's at your own risk, understand.'

Jenna nodded. 'Understood.' She wanted to take Adam's hand, but she couldn't do that here. Instead she turned quickly, finding that he was standing right behind her, and was too late to stop herself bumping into him.

'Okay.' His hand on her arm reassured her. 'I'll go in, and you can take the casualties as they come out.' He gave her arm a squeeze and made his way over to the fire truck.

'Correction. We both go in.' She muttered the words at him as he climbed up into the cabin. He might be able to intimidate the site manager, but he didn't scare her.

'No, Jen.' He didn't even look at her.

'You can't stop me.'

'I can ask you.' He'd turned to face her now.

'Yes, and I can tell you to go and boil your head. Is someone going to die just because you're too pig-headed to let me go in there and save them?'

He pressed his lips together. 'I'll speak to Parker, make sure that there's someone in there who's responsible for your safety. You stick with him and do as he says. Right?'

Jenna's heart sank. Adam still couldn't trust himself enough to be the one to look after her. And he was the only person she wanted, the only one she needed. She took the yellow hard hat that he passed down from the cabin and dumped it on her head, finding that it was too big and needed some adjustment.

'Right, Jenna? Do we have a deal?' He wasn't going to let her get away without a reply.

'Yes. Deal. We have a deal.'

CHAPTER ELEVEN

It was hot, heavy work, and Jenna's thick jacket and boots were only making it worse. But she kept them on, sweating under the morning sun, which was just beginning to break into the filthy space that was still filled with choking dust.

They were inside the shell of a building. Two floors above them, the retaining walls were still standing, but the roof was off and the floors had collapsed through. On the far side of the ground floor the fire crew worked, steady and untiring, on a pile of rubble, which had obviously come from an internal wall.

The first man had been uncovered and she and Adam were let in close to do their work. Almost before he was strapped firmly to a gurney and carried out to the waiting ambulance, there was a second. And then a third. As Adam knelt beside him, the fire crew kept working, clearing the last of the rubble, to make sure that there was no one else.

'He's dead, Adam.' Jenna was standing behind him, but it was obvious the man was dead. Massive cranial destruction, his chest a mess of bloody pulp.

'Yeah.' Adam had still examined the body, as if there was some hope that it was possible to rebuild a man who had been shattered almost beyond recognition. He turned, and caught the ever-present Parker's eye. 'I'm pronouncing this man dead. Radio it in.'

There would be another ambulance here in a moment and they could be diverted to tend to the living. Even though the man was dead beyond any doubt or question, the fire crew would have been bound to wait for the paramedics and keep working as if he were alive, unless he was pronounced dead by a doctor.

Parker nodded and got on his radio. 'We'll check the rest, make sure there's no one else, and then get out of here. I don't like the look of this floor.' He turned to Jenna. 'You might want to wait outside.'

The words stung but it was a purely operational judgement. Adam was stronger than she was, and could help the fire crew dig. She was just an extra one-hundred-and-twenty-five pounds' worth of stress on the floor, which wasn't strictly necessary at the moment.

'Go.' Adam's voice brooked no argument. 'I'll stay and help them check the rest of the area, and I'll be with you in a moment.'

Parker was sending all but one of the rest of the fire crew out as well. Three men were needed and two of them would be Adam and himself. Jenna hesitated and then nodded, walking over to fetch the medical bag that had been dumped in the far corner of the space.

There was a grinding sound and the floor juddered sickeningly beneath her feet. 'Freeze!' Parker's voice was quiet but unmistakeably an order. Jenna froze. Looking around, she saw Parker and Adam over by the rubble and another member of the fire crew by the exit door, all caught in suspended animation. The floor seemed to have tipped and was suddenly at an angle.

'Easy. Stay still.' Adam's eyes were fixed on hers. Not letting her go. As if somehow his gaze was a lifeline that would reel her in, save her from whatever danger it was that Parker had seen.

There was a sudden crack, and noise and dust choked her senses. She saw Adam's face, a snapshot of agony, and then she was falling.

Adam watched in horror as the floor tilted, seemingly in slow motion, and seemed to buckle under Jenna's feet as she shifted the heavy medical bag. She was still now, in response to Parker's order, her eyes fixed on his face. In the silence, the rumble of traffic in the distance seemed suddenly to grow into a deafening din.

The floor was shaking, as if in response to some over-whelming force, and the sound of a train on the railway line behind the site reached his ears. All of his nerves were screaming at him to run to her, but he knew that would only increase the weight on the floor where she was stand-ing. He forced himself to keep his voice steady and quiet, and hoped that she wouldn't move.

She didn't move but the floor did. There was a deaf-ening crack and Jenna disappeared from view through a gaping hole in the floor. Adam felt Parker's hand on his arm, holding him back, but he shook himself free.

'Stay back. I'll go.' Parker rapped out the quiet order.

Like hell he would. Adam heard Parker's muttered curse behind him as he slid across the floor and reached the edge of the hole. She was down there, curled up, knees almost to her chin, her arms protectively over her head. Good girl. She wasn't moving, but Adam could hear her whimpering quietly, in fear, pain or both.

'Behind you. Watch out.' Parker's urgent voice made Adam look around. Some of the debris on the floor was beginning to slide towards the steeper incline at the rim of the hole. A pane of glass leant carefully up against one wall fell and shattered, scattering shards across the floor.

Afraid that if he called out to her she might move her head out of the protective cradle of her arms, Adam quickly let himself down through the hole, jumping the final few feet and throwing himself towards her.

'Get away from the hole.' Adam could hear Parker's voice, rising above the sound of sliding debris above his head. There was no time to assess her injuries. He had to move her now, before they were crushed together beneath a pile of masonry. He picked her up and she screamed, fingers grappling for a hold around his neck.

It was pain, not fear. Adam had heard both before, and she was in pain. He prayed that it wasn't her spine. Running for the back wall of the space, he put her down against it as gently as he could and threw himself over her.

There was a moment of silence, broken only by the groaning of overstressed timbers and the ominous rumble of something moving above them. He cradled her head against his chest, talking to her in the hope that she could hear him. 'Jenna. It's okay, honey. You're okay.' It wasn't medical opinion, just agonised hope. She had to be okay.

She moved under him, and his heart almost burst. 'Adam.' She was conscious, airway clear. And it was his name that she called.

'Okay. It's all going to be okay. Just hang in there.' The roar of falling masonry blocked everything else out as rubble crashed down, bringing half of the ceiling along with it. Something hit his back, then again, a blow that took his breath away, but he didn't care. If fate was going to dictate that only one of them made it out of here alive, all he could do was make sure it was her.

'Adam. I'm okay, it's just my leg.' She was squirming

under him, crying his name, but he held her fast, preventing her from moving from the shelter of his body. The stream of debris slowed to a shower of dust.

'Status. Adam, your status.' Parker's low, urgent call reached his ears.

'She's hurt. Can't tell how badly yet.' The words seared through him as he called.

'And you?'

'Fine.' Adam looked around quickly, his eyes becoming accustomed to the gloom. They were in a large basement room, one side of which was completely full of collapsed brickwork. What was left of the ceiling over their heads was groaning, and little streams of dust were trickling downwards. He needed to get her out of here before the whole thing came down on them.

'Okay. Can you get out of that room, towards the back of the building? It's more stable there.'

Adam scanned the walls. 'Yes, there's a door. I don't know where it leads.'

'Find out. Now, before any more of this comes down.'

Adam got to his feet, feeling his back pull as he did so. Bending to gather her up in his arms, he heard her groan in pain. 'Sorry, honey. Just hang in there a little longer.'

'Do it, Adam. I'm okay.' She clung to him, nestling into his shoulder, and he gasped for air. She wasn't okay, but she was trusting him to take care of her. He would do anything, everything to do just that.

He nudged the door open with his foot, turning sideways to her through it. The room beyond was smaller, darker, but the ceiling seemed undamaged. It had obviously served as some kind of stockroom as there were racks on the walls and an old desk and chair, with an area of carpeting at the far end. Adam carried her through, laying her carefully down on the floor.

'That's better. Thanks.' Her voice was steadier now, none of the slurring associated with concussion. She tried to move and he quieted her.

'Stay still, Jen. Please, just for a minute.' He found her hand and clasped it. 'I'm going to call up to Parker.'

He moved quickly over to the door, feeling for his phone in his pocket and flipping it open, checking it was undamaged and that he had a signal. Calling the number out, he heard Parker repeating it back to him.

'Got it.'

'Give me five minutes. I need to see how she is. I'm putting my mobile on to vibrate.' Adam didn't want the shrill tones of his phone dislodging anything else.

'Right you are. I'm going around the back to see if there's a way down to you, but I'll leave a man up here. Call up if you need anything.'

'Thanks.' Adam moved back into the gloom, to where Jenna was lying on the floor, still. He knelt down beside her and took her hand. 'Okay, honey. You know the drill.'

'Yes. Airway clear.' She managed a laugh. 'Clear enough to ask you what the hell you're doing down here.'

He chuckled, unzipping her jacket and slipping his hands inside. 'I'm a sucker for women covered in grime. Didn't I tell you?'

'Not that I remember. But I'll keep it in mind.' Her sharp intake of breath told him that he'd found a sore spot and he stopped, investigating carefully.

'Maybe a cracked rib. Deep breath.'

She obediently took the breath. 'It's okay. I think I hit my side when I fell. Probably just bruised.' One hand moved to her wrist and she felt for her pulse.

'Will you stop that? That's my job. Did you hit your head?'

'No. And my pulse is steady.'

Adam checked anyway. Her heart was beating more strongly and steadily than his was. He ran his hands over her hips, pressing gently. 'Any pain in your hips and back?'

'No. My ankle hurts.'

'Okay, first things first.' He checked her chest and back thoroughly, feeling for any signs of injury. 'Can you taste any blood in your mouth?'

'No. Just dust.' He felt her hand on his arm. 'It's just my ankle, Adam. I'm okay apart from that.'

He chuckled into the gloom. 'Stop self-diagnosing.'

'I'm not. I'm telling you my symptoms. My ankle hurts.' He could hear the pain in her voice now and she shifted, feeling for the pocket of her jacket. 'Here. Will you take a look at it for me?' She pressed something into his hand.

'Where did you get this?' It was a small torch.

'I keep it in my bag for when I come home late at night. I slipped it in my pocket when I got dressed this morning, thought it might come in handy.'

Adam grinned into the darkness. 'Good thought.' He flipped the torch on, directing the beam away from her face. It was powerful, even if it was small. Adam wondered how long the batteries would last. Setting it down on the floor, he turned to her. Her face was covered in grime and streaked with tears. 'Hey, there, beautiful.'

'Hey, yourself.' Her voice was laced with pain now that the adrenaline in her system had spiked and dropped. She nodded down towards her feet. 'Right ankle.'

'Okay, lie still. Let's take a look.' Adam took his jacket off, folding it into a makeshift pillow, and carefully cut the laces of her boot, opening it as wide as he could. 'You know the next line, don't you?'

'Yes. This may hurt a little, but I'll be as quick as I can.'

He cut through as much of the boot as he could, and then carefully pulled it off.

It would have been better if she'd screamed, cursed him, anything. But Adam couldn't block out the whimper of agony as he carefully laid her foot down on his folded jacket and swiftly cut her sock away to expose her ankle.

'How does it look?' She was sitting up now, speaking between gritted teeth, and he turned, wrapping his arms around her, holding her tight, as he rubbed her back gently.

'I think it's broken. I…I'm sorry, Jen. It must have hurt like hell when I picked you up.'

She snuffled into his chest. 'Don't be such a wuss. If you hadn't then I wouldn't be feeling anything right now.'

She was right but that didn't make him feel any better. She couldn't have moved fast enough to get out of the way of the pile of masonry that had come through the hole in the ceiling. But all the same he'd handled her roughly and she hadn't complained once. He pressed her to his chest. 'You're going to be just fine, Jen.'

'I know. I'm glad you're here. Even if I am angry with you for coming after me like that, landing yourself in this situation.'

He hadn't even thought about that. As far as he was concerned, the best place for him was by her side. It was the only place, and instinct had dictated that before reasoning had confirmed it. He bent and brushed a brief kiss across her lips. She tasted of brick dust and strawberries.

'No place I'd rather be.' It wasn't just some meaningless pleasantry, it was a binding vow. He'd stay with her, come hell or high water, until she was out of there. And he'd keep her safe with the last breath in his body. It wasn't a matter of choice or decision, that was just how things were.

* * *

He was holding her tightly, his heart beating fast against her cheek. She could almost, almost but not quite, block out the pain in her leg when she was in his arms. No, scratch that. It hurt. It was just more bearable when he was holding her.

She half felt, half heard his phone, vibrating in his pocket. He pulled it out, keeping her supported against his body with his free hand. Someone was on the other end, speaking quickly, and Adam listened, giving only short acknowledgements to let the other person know he'd heard and understood.

'She's okay. Probable broken ankle, but apart from that she's good.' Jenna felt his arm tighten around her. 'Can you get some medical supplies down to us? Good.' He reeled off a list of what he wanted, and Jenna's heart sank. It sounded as if they were going to be down here for a while, if he needed all that.

'Okay, thanks.' Adam paused. 'If you hear how the two casualties are, will you let me know? Yeah, thanks. Wait a minute, will you?' He let the phone drop from his ear. 'Jen, do you have your phone on you?'

'Yes.' He loosened his grip on her slightly, just enough to allow her to feel in her pocket. 'It's here.'

'Okay, check if it's working and how much battery time you've got left.'

She thumbed a key and the display lit up. 'Yeah, I've got three bars on reception and it's practically fully charged.' She dialled the speaking clock and listened carefully. 'Yes, it's fine.'

'Good.' He recited her number slowly into his phone. 'My battery's low, so if you can't get me, call Jenna.' He nodded into the phone and grinned. 'Thanks, Parker. Much appreciated.' He snapped the phone closed and wound his other arm around her shoulders. 'Okay. We're good.'

'What did he say?' It hadn't sounded all that good.

'They can't get to us from where you fell, the floor's far too unstable for them to work on. But they know where we are, and the structure above us looks much more stable. There's a staircase at the back of the building and they're coming that way, but it's full of rubble from the demolition and clearing it might take a while.'

'How long?'

'I don't know. It won't be five minutes, but it won't be all day. Somewhere in between. I'm sorry, Jen.'

'Don't be.' Jenna took a breath, trying to steady her nerves. 'We'll just sit tight and wait, yes?'

'Yeah. And meanwhile, there are some things on their way to make you more comfortable.'

It took fifteen minutes for the bag to come down to them. Adam had made her as comfortable as he could, carefully elevating the leg and propping it up on a wooden box, his jacket still folded under it. The basement was cool, and when he laid her down flat she began to shiver so he held her, supporting her body against his. He rubbed her back, massaged her neck, the tops of her legs and even the palms of her hands. It was unconventional, but it seemed to work. With the tension gone from her body, and warm and safe in his arms, the pain receded a little.

Finally, Adam's phone rang. He answered it, listened for a moment and then turned to her. 'I'll be one minute.'

She couldn't bear for him to go out there. It wasn't safe. Jenna clung to him, imploring him silently to stay.

'One minute, I promise. Count it off.' He laid the phone down on the floor and took her by the shoulders. 'Parker's up there, keeping an eye on things.'

She didn't care that the line was open, and that whoever was on the other end could probably hear her. 'No,

Adam. I don't need anything in that bag, not as much as I need you in one piece and here with me.'

He brushed a kiss against her lips. 'It's okay. Trust me, Jen. I'll be back.' Adam felt for the torch, switched it back on and picked up the phone. 'Sixty. Fifty-nine…count with me.'

'Fifty-eight. Fifty-seven.' He rose and quickly made his way towards the door, pushing it open and looking upwards. Then he disappeared.

'Forty. Thirty-nine.' She was beginning to cry, straining her ears for the sound of anything that might mean that he was in trouble out there.

'Nineteen. Eighteen.' He appeared in the doorway, a large bag in one hand, and a bench mattress from an ambulance, rolled around red blankets and a pillow. Depositing them on the floor next to her, he lifted his phone to his ear and spoke into it.

'All right. Thanks, Parker… Yeah, okay, I understand. Don't rush it, we're okay to sit tight.' He cut the line, and stuffed the phone back into his pocket.

'What did he say?'

'It'll be at least a couple of hours, more likely three before they can get to us. There's a lot of rubble between them and us.'

'You told him not to take any risks with the men, though, didn't you? We can wait.'

'I told him. Now, let's get you sorted.'

He unrolled the mattress, sliding it carefully under her, and Jenna relaxed back onto it. Unzipping the bag, he rummaged around inside and brought out a lantern torch, switching it on and bathing the whole room with light. A bottle of water followed and he used a little to sluice the worst of the grime from his hands then washed them with cleansing gel. Pulling out a cardboard box, he took out a blister pack containing a syringe.

'Oh, no, you don't.' Anything that touched the searing pain in her leg was going to make her feel drowsy. Which would mean he couldn't leave her alone.

'Jen, are you seriously going to tell me that your leg doesn't hurt you?' He stopped what he was doing and knelt beside her.

'No. But I need to keep my wits about me.'

The look of hurt on his face was palpable, slamming against her senses, making her forget for a moment about the pain in her leg. 'You trust me so little.' It was the resignation in his voice that hurt most.

'I trust you so much I know you'd never leave me alone if you'd just given me a shot of morphine.' She jutted her chin aggressively. It was the only way to get through the frustration of him continually questioning himself.

He caught on, and something like hope sparked in his eyes. Jenna could have cried at the cruelty of it all. 'I won't leave you with a broken ankle. I wouldn't leave you with a broken fingernail. That's non-negotiable.'

'But…but suppose…' Jenna was casting around in her mind to find some scenario that might mean he'd have to leave her behind. That he could get out of here before she could, while she waited for the fire crew.

'Suppose nothing. I'm not going anywhere and that's final. And since I'm stuck here with you, I'd rather you were comfortable and not biting my head off because you're in pain. What do you say?'

Warmth flooded through her. Like the heat from the injection he was about to give her, but far more potent. 'Okay. How good are you with finding a vein, then?'

He shrugged cheerfully, rolling up the sleeve of her

jacket. 'Guess you're about to find out. Taking any other medication?'

'You know I'm not.'

'Previous contra-indications? Asthma, Kidney...?'

'No! Just give me the pain control, will you?'

'That's more like it.' He put on a pair of gloves, snapping them theatrically, swabbed her arm and slid the needle in first time. 'How's that?'

'Not bad.' Warmth was beginning to spread along her arm.

'I thought that was pretty near perfect myself.' He disposed of the syringe and sat next to her on the floor, holding her hand while the morphine kicked in. 'Feeling better?'

'Yes. Thanks.' She knew now what it felt like when that smile spread across a patient's face. The relief when pain receded into the background was pleasure in itself. Something like what she felt when she was with Adam.

The object of her rose-tinted speculations was busying himself, carefully cutting the leg of her jeans to the knee, powdering her ankle and carefully slipping an inflatable splint over her foot. 'Can you feel that?' He was gently tapping her toes.

'Hmm? Yes.' She smiled at Adam. 'Thoughtful of them to put powder in the bag.'

He chuckled. 'Yeah.' He propped a cushion gently behind her head. 'Comfortable?'

'Yes, comfortable. Come here.'

CHAPTER TWELVE

SHE was beginning to drift slightly. Not so much that she couldn't still think for herself, he'd made sure to give her a low dose so that he could give her more if needed. But the pain receptors in her brain were zoning away from her ankle, which was just what he wanted them to do. If he couldn't get her out of this basement, the least he could do was to help her concentrate on something else.

He gave her some water and used some of the antiseptic wipes to clean her face and hands. He was probably using more of their limited supply than was strictly sensible, but it seemed to give her comfort that even now they were a long way from doing just what was strictly necessary. He stretched out on the carpet next to her, arranging the blanket over her body.

'I don't need that, I'm too hot. Fold it up and put it underneath you.' He felt her hands and foot and she was warm enough. He slid the blanket away from her, and folded it up.

'Better?' His own back was aching now, but that didn't matter. It didn't matter that he could still feel a stickiness right where the top of his jeans met his spine. The bleeding had stopped now, and he wouldn't show her that he was hurt. And he wouldn't leave her alone, take the surgical tape that was in the bag, and apply it out of her sight. There was time enough for that later.

'Yes.' She looked up at him. 'Thanks, Adam.'

'My pleasure.' He picked up the water bottle. 'You want a little more to drink?'

She made him drink first, and he took a couple of sips from the bottle, grateful for the moisture in his throat. She drank a little, screwing the top back on to the bottle. 'How much longer do you reckon?'

He looked at his watch. 'A couple of hours at least. If Parker hasn't called me by then, I'll give him a ring, see what's up.'

She nodded and he rolled onto his back, shifting the folded blanket underneath his head. That was better. His back didn't hurt as much now. Casually he pulled one knee up slightly to stretch it a little and as the arch of his back touched the floor, he winced.

'What?' She was suddenly alert.

'Nothing.'

'I distinctly heard a sharp intake of breath.'

'I thought I felt a moth on my face.'

'Crap.' She was up on one elbow, now. 'What was it, or do I have to strip you to find out?'

He grinned up at the ceiling. Even here, even now, the thought didn't seem like a bad one.

'Adam, do you want me to come after you? I will, you know.'

'You can't. I'm faster than you at the moment.'

'I'll still try.' A small sound escaped her throat as she twisted round, trying to catch hold of his arm.

'Stop it.'

She ignored him. Pulling herself up into a sitting position, she leaned farther over, and he caught her arms before she collapsed onto his chest. 'Stop it, Jen. Since when

did the meaning of immobilise become so hard to understand?' Her face was contorted with determination and
pain. 'Okay, okay.' He guided her back onto the mattress
and turned, wincing as he pulled his sweater and shirt up
over his head.

'Adam. For goodness' sake, why didn't you tell me?'

He sighed. 'It didn't feel too bad up till now. It just
caught me when I lay on my back.' It was true. He'd been
so concerned for her that he hadn't even realised he was
in pain.

'I'm not surprised, you've got glass in there.' She had
picked up the lantern and was shining it onto his back.
'Go and get the bag, will you? And do you have a pair of
tweezers in your penknife?'

'Yeah.' He passed her his penknife and rose to fetch
the bag. He sat back down, his back to her, while she rummaged inside it, bringing out gloves, sterile wipes and
water. 'Ow! Go easy there.'

'Serves you right. Keep still, will you?'

'Fine bedside manner you've got. Remind me never to
be carted into Casualty when you're on shift. Ow, Jenna!'

'Be quiet.' They both knew that she was being as gentle as she could, but it felt good to let off a little steam.
He felt a trickle of water on his back, and shadows swung
back and forth on the wall in front of him as she tilted the
torch, making sure there were no shards of glass left in
the wound.

'Okay, that's it. When exactly did you think you were
going to do something about this?'

'Later. I can't see the small of my back, I'm not double-
jointed.'

She giggled. 'That's not what you said—'

'Enough!' It was bad enough being here like this, her

laughter echoing in his ears, her fingers on his skin. 'Be a bit professional, can't you?'

He felt her lips brush his spine. 'A minute ago you were complaining about my bedside manner.'

'Well, you're supposed to put your patients at ease, not attack them and then make a pass at them.'

She huffed a short breath. 'I resign, then. Consider me officially no longer your doctor and pass me the surgical tape, please. I'll just put some gauze on it and leave it open so they can wash it out properly later on.'

He chuckled. 'You can't resign. I'm sacking you.' He dropped the tape into her hand, and felt her fingers on his back again. 'Gross misconduct.'

'Watch it. You want misconduct, I'll give you misconduct.' She ran her fingers down his spine, making him shiver with pleasure. 'Hold it, don't turn around yet.'

He felt her thumb higher on his back and winced. He hadn't even felt that cut until now. She washed and dressed it, and tapped his shoulder. 'You can turn around now. And give me your shirt.'

He turned, and saw her eyes, bright with humour, scanning his body candidly. 'Cut it out.' He grinned at her, making no move to pull his shirt back on.

'A girl can look, can't she?'

'She can do whatever she likes.' He leaned in slightly, and she pulled him the rest of the way. The kiss was nothing to do with the memories of their nights together and everything to do with reassurance, a solemn promise that he would care for her and keep her from harm. For the time being, anyway.

She was the first to break the spell. Catching up his shirt, she held it up to the light, examining it carefully. 'I just want to make sure there's no glass in here.'

'Careful. Don't cut your fingers.' He couldn't keep his eyes off her.

'It's okay. Look, there's just a tiny bit there, can you get it out?'

Adam reached for the tweezers and disposed of the piece of glass, caught in the threads of his shirt. Taking it from her, he pulled it back over his head. 'I guess we'd better switch the light off. Conserve the battery.'

She caught his hand. 'Okay. Just keep hold of me, eh?'

'Don't want you running out on me in the dark.' He flipped the torch off and lay down next to her, his head resting on the soft folds of the blanket. 'Now that the lights are out, do you want a story?'

'Mmm. That would be nice.'

'Okay. Are you sitting comfortably?'

'Yes.'

'Then I'll begin. Once upon a time, in a land far away, where hummingbirds will feed from your hand...' The sound of bumps and falling debris reached his ears, but Adam didn't stop. He told her stories about his work, his patients, the communities he'd visited. The smile in her voice when she commented kept him talking, trying to weave a spell that would banish her fears and some of her pain.

'So what happened to the goat?'

'Oh, the goat was all right. Goats are very resilient creatures, they take most things in their stride.'

'And the bride's mother?'

He shrugged, one hand finding her cheek so that he could brush the backs of his fingers against it. 'She got over it. The groom's uncle promised to rebuild her veranda and when we went back the following year, everyone had forgotten about it. I helped deliver the couple's first child.'

'That's nice. So everything worked out, then?' She

turned her head so that her lips came into brief contact with his fingers.

'Yeah. Everything worked out.' They lay in silence for a while, holding hands, until a buzz from his pocket roused Adam.

It was Parker, and he had good news. Adam snapped his phone closed and reached for the torch. 'Cover your eyes a moment, I'm just going to switch the light back on. They're almost through.'

He was blinded for a moment and then began to make out her face, shining with happiness. 'Go and see, Adam.'

'No. Parker said we should wait here. He doesn't want to worry that we're on the other side when they push through the last of the rubble.' He sat up, stretching his limbs. 'Just be patient. It won't be much longer.'

It seemed to be longer than the time they'd spent in the darkness, talking together, but in reality it was just a few minutes. The sound of footsteps echoed along the corridor, and two grimy, burly figures appeared in the doorway.

'Hi, guys.' Jenna propped herself up on one elbow and gave them a smile of pure joy. 'Good to see you.'

It wasn't that she was sorry to be rescued, but Jenna was still aware of having lost something. Those few hours, when the only person she'd had in the world had been Adam. And she had been the only one in his world. It was almost an intrusion when two of the fire crew appeared in the doorway.

Adam jumped to his feet, striding over to them and shaking their hands. There was a brief exchange of words over the shortwave radio, and then the two came to squat down next to Jenna.

'Comfortable, then?' One of them enquired cheerily.

'Yes, thanks. Thought I'd sit it out while you did all the work.' Jenna joked off the pain in her leg.

'Wise lady.' The fireman was looking at her leg. 'Now, we just need to decide how best to get you out of here.' He looked up at Adam. 'A stretcher's out of the question, and it'll take a while to get things clear enough to get a chair down here. I think our best bet is to carry her.'

Adam nodded. Jenna knew that time was everything. More time, more risk, to both her and Adam and the fire crew. 'Yes, let's get out of here, guys.'

She felt for Adam's hand. She wanted him to take her out of here but she couldn't ask. He was tired and hurt, he would be better leaving it to one of the firemen.

'I'll take her.' There was no mistaking the possessiveness in his voice.

A brief querying glance between the two firemen was quickly suppressed as she reached for Adam, winding her arms around his neck. He'd come down here to get her. It was his right to take her out, if he wanted to, and the fact that he did warmed her.

'Okay, mate. Fair enough.' The fireman backed off. He knew what Adam had done, too. 'Let's be quick about it, though.'

Adam slipped his arms under her back and legs. 'Okay, you know the next line, don't you?'

She grinned at him. 'This is going to hurt a little, but I'll be as quick as I can.'

'You've got it. Hang in there, honey, we're nearly there.'

The morphine was beginning to wear off a little, and her ankle hurt much more than a little when Adam lifted her. Jenna hung on to him, squeezing her eyes shut, trying not to cry as he carefully carried her through twists and turns and then climbed a staircase, following the firemen's quickly worded directions. She heard the noise of the street and felt the breeze on her face and opened her eyes.

Parker was there, grinning at her and motioning Adam towards the ambulance stretcher that stood ready. Adam had kept his promise. He'd said they'd get out together and they had. Tears started to well up again and she buried her head in the crook of his shoulder, hanging on to him as gentle hands laid her down on the stretcher.

'Hey, Jen. Trying us out to see what the ride's like?' It was Joel, with Andy by his side, grinning.

She tried to reply, make a joke back at him, but the words wouldn't come. Only tears, and she covered her face, ashamed at her sudden loss of control, there in front of everyone.

She felt Adam's hand on her shoulder, squeezing gently. 'Brave lady, this one. Took a fifteen-foot fall, a broken ankle and being shut away with me in the dark for a couple of hours without a single complaint.'

Parker laughed. 'Ted, do you hear that?' Jenna took her hands away from her face in time to see him gesture towards one of the crew. 'He tripped over a hose and broke his arm last year and bawled like a baby.'

A ripple of laughter surged around the men, and Adam produced a medical wipe from his pocket, handing it to her. Jenna blew her nose and managed a smile.

'Nice job.' Parker took her hand and gave it a shake. 'I heard about the two men who were taken to hospital and they're going to be okay. One of them was touch and go for a while, and the guy I spoke to at the hospital said that if you hadn't given him medical attention on site, he wouldn't have made it.'

At least they'd managed to achieve something by being there. Jenna only had the chance to squeeze Parker's hand

and mouth a silent 'Thank you' before she was on the move, being lifted into the ambulance.

Adam climbed in behind her as Joel secured the stretcher securely in place. 'You'll be staying a couple of minutes?'

'Yep. Just to get everything sorted. Are you coming with us?'

Adam nodded. 'Don't go without me.' He turned to Jenna. 'Something I have to do first.' He gestured back towards the fire crew, who were drifting away to form a group around the back of the fire truck. 'I'll be right back.'

'Go. Tell them thanks from me, too.'

'Of course.' Adam flashed her a grin as he ducked back out of the ambulance and hurried over to the group of men. Jenna saw him shake each man's hand, and the small group turned in her direction, their thumbs-up signals telling Jenna that Adam had done as she'd asked.

'Lie down, will you?' Joel was grinning at her. 'Just pretend you're the patient for a minute.'

'Wait.' Jenna batted him away and watched as Adam hurried back.

'Can you do anything with this one? We've got a struggler on our hands.' Joel turned to Adam.

'Nope.' Adam was grinning broadly. 'You might have to sedate her.'

Jenna lay back on the trolley. It was narrow but soft and comfortable and now that Adam was there there was no need to keep straining to sit up. Her whole body ached, and she began to wonder how many bruises she had. It felt like one very big one at the moment.

'Okay. Just relax.' Joel was in medic mode and she felt him clip the pulse monitor on to her finger. 'Has she had any pain relief?'

Adam leant over, unpinning the note that he'd written

and secured to the front of her jacket. 'Here. Time and dosage.' In case anything had happened to him, then they'd know immediately what drugs she'd had and when.

Joel nodded. 'Okay. Jen, how much pain have you got? One to ten.'

'Three and a bit.'

'Yeah, looks like a big bit. You're very pale. Do you want something more?'

'Yes. Thanks.' She relaxed back into the small pillow and closed her eyes. She let them get on with it, feeling the cool swab on her arm and the prick of a needle. Adam's fingers brushed hers and then closed firmly around them. Good. Everything was good.

CHAPTER THIRTEEN

EACH bump in the road jarred Adam's aching limbs, but he didn't let go of her hand, even when it seemed that she was sleeping. He knew she wasn't. The way she gripped him, her fingers wound around his tightly, told him so.

She was safe. It had been the only thing he could think about in that basement. How to keep her safe. How to get her out of there. And he'd done it. Not without a great deal of help, but he'd been the one she had clung to and he hadn't let her down. Adam's limbs shook at the thought.

Joel tried to get him to submit to a cursory examination and backed off when Adam refused. He was obviously good at what he did and knew when to insist and when to leave it be. All Adam wanted to do was to stay with Jenna, keep the promise he'd made, the one that was his only reason for being at the moment.

She stirred as they lifted her down from the ambulance and he had to let go of her hand. 'Still here. We won't both fit through those doors together.'

'Hmm. Okay.' As soon as they were out of the ambulance and through the doors to A and E he caught up and took her hand in his again. Joel waved him over to a nearby chair and he shook his head, receiving a slight shrug in return.

'All right, what have we here, then?' Rob's voice penetrated his consciousness, and Adam breathed a sigh of relief. Jenna was going to be seen right away.

'Rob.' She opened her eyes and smiled up at him. 'Don't you have anything better to do?'

'Not at the moment. Thought I'd come and see what kind of dog's dinner Adam's managed to make of your ankle.' Rob grinned at Adam as he helped wheel the trolley over to a cubicle.

'I'm not jumping the queue.' Jenna's lips were pressed together.

'Quite right. You aren't. We've got a couple of minor cuts and someone who's been gummed by a toothless poodle out there. Do the math.' Rob grinned down at her. 'Okay, what have we got?' He turned to Adam. 'Want to sit down, old man?'

In other words get out of the way. Adam eased himself into the chair beside Jenna's trolley, one hand resting on the rail at the side. Anything to keep some kind of contact with her. He watched as Rob gingerly felt along Jenna's arms and legs and he jumped as she winced.

'Please…' His lips formed the words but they were no more than a whisper. How many times had he heard that from people as he had examined his patients? Please don't hurt her. He knew that Rob was doing what he had to do, but watching him do this was almost more than he could bear.

'Look.' Rob turned on him. 'You're filthy. I don't want you near my patient until you've cleaned up. Go and take a shower.' Rob felt in his pocket. 'Here are the keys to my locker.'

Rob was right. He was more than qualified to do whatever Jenna needed. He flipped his gaze to Jenna and she turned her beautiful blue eyes on him. 'Go on. I'll be here when you get back.'

* * *

When Adam returned to the cubicle, wearing a clean T-shirt from Rob's locker, she was propped up on the bed, watching as Rob examined her ankle. Her face was pale, but she managed a smile when she saw him.

'Hey, there. Okay?'

'That's my line, isn't it?'

'Oh, and can't a girl enquire? Don't hog it all to yourself.'

Adam grinned at the flash of defiant humour. Jenna winced as Rob gently probed her ankle and Adam almost turned on him in rage. He knew Rob was only doing his job, but did he have to hurt her?

He forced himself to perch on the edge of the seat by the bed and reached for her hand. If that was the role he was consigned to then he'd better get on with it. Someone had cleaned her hands and face, but she still had a smudge of grime over her eyebrow.

'They've missed a bit.' He took a wipe from the box by the bed and gestured towards her brow. 'Close your eyes.'

He'd said that last night, and the brief twist of her mouth before she obeyed him told Adam that she remembered it, too. Carefully, he cleaned the dirt from her face, brushing her hair back from her forehead.

'Can I have something to drink?' She was asking him, not Rob, but Adam gritted his teeth and turned towards Rob.

'Yeah, just some water.' Rob resumed his inspection of Jenna's leg and Adam hurried to fetch some water from the cooler.

She sipped the water slowly, nestling in the crook of his arm as he supported her back. Rob turned, seemingly satisfied with his examination.

'Right, Jenna. It appears that through a miracle of modern guesswork Adam has correctly diagnosed the fact that you have a broken ankle and a number of rather nasty bruises.' He pointed to her eye. 'Looks as if you'll have a shiner in the morning.'

She grinned at him. 'Yeah, I reckoned as much. Thanks, Rob.'

'My pleasure.' Rob rounded on Adam. 'Next…'

Jenna giggled. 'I sneaked on you, Adam. Better show him those cuts.'

'They're okay.'

Rob rolled his eyes. 'So which speech do you want? The one about doctors thinking that they're different from every other mortal on the planet because they don't need medical treatment, or the one about untended cuts? I'll set Brenda on you if you're not careful and she's been taking tae kwon do classes.'

'She's quite good at it. You'll be flat on your face in an arm lock before you know what's hit you.' Jenna's eyes were twinkling and a little of the colour had returned to her face. 'She's not on duty today, though, is she, Rob?'

'On her way in. I called her just before you two arrived.' Rob grimaced at Adam. 'So which is it, then? My healing hands or a well-placed smack on the jaw from Brenda?'

Adam sat down quickly on the stool that Rob had indicated, keeping his eyes on Jenna. 'Have you ordered the X-rays yet? What about pain relief?'

Adam could feel Rob probing his back, and he suddenly ripped off the dressing that Adam had hastily applied after he'd got out of the shower. 'Never thought of that. Might not be a bad idea. What do you say, Jen?'

'Dunno.' Jenna's gaze was on him, a little bleary, but right now her eyes were the most beautiful things in the world. She patted his hand reassuringly. 'It's all done. They'll be along in a minute to take us over there.'

'I'll have a snap of your ribs while they're at it.' Rob's voice brooked no argument. 'Breathe.'

Adam complied, wincing when he felt Rob's fingers around his rib cage. 'Yeah. Sorry, mate.'

Rob snorted. 'Don't sweat it. You should have seen me when Ellie and Daisy were born.'

'We were contemplating giving the midwife a break and sedating him.' Jenna was smiling, holding his hand. Making jokes. She was okay. 'Doctors are always the worst. We know all the things that can happen.' She gave a little nod to emphasise the point.

All the things that could have happened. If he hadn't been able to move Jenna out of the way of the crushing debris falling towards her through that hole in the floor. If she'd been badly hurt when she'd fallen. If she'd died, like Elena. Adam took a deep breath. It hadn't happened, and that was all there was to it.

'Hey.' She was tapping her finger on his hand, the way she did when the rage took him. It was okay. She didn't need to. He'd been angry, fearful, all those things, but that was different. Normal and under control. The blind rage that paralysed him and took away his very being when it hit had not surfaced.

'It's okay.' He nodded to her, a silent acknowledgement that he was still there. Still caught in her enchanting blue eyes.

'Keep still, will you?' Rob seemed to be pretty much done with him now. 'I'll tape those cuts, but they look fine. How Jenna managed to get all the glass out by torchlight and with a broken ankle and a dose of morphine in her system I'll never know.'

'She's good.' Adam saw the warmth bloom in her eyes at his words.

'Few of us have a right to be that good.' Rob was taping and dressing the wound and when he'd finished, he slapped Adam on the shoulder. 'Done.'

Adam turned and gave him a nod. 'Cheers. Thanks for everything, Rob.'

'No problem.' Rob folded his arms, looking back and forth between Adam and Jenna. He was obviously still in professional mode. 'I'm thinking of discharging you both, only I don't want Jenna on her own tonight. She needs someone to keep an eye on her.'

'That's okay. I'll be there.' Adam tried to make it sound as if he was volunteering for the duty on medical grounds, and saw Jenna nodding quietly out of the corner of his eye.

'Fair enough. Assuming that the X-rays don't show up anything unexpected, we'll put a temporary cast on Jen's leg and then you can both go.' A tone sounded from Rob's pocket and he stripped off his surgical gloves and pulled his phone out. 'That's Brenda. She's here now and she's checked on the wait for the X-rays and it'll be another half-hour.'

'That's okay. May I have some more water, please?' Jenna looked at Rob imploringly and he nodded.

'Sure. Brenda's got you some fresh clothes and I think she's planning on helping you clean up a bit.' Jenna's look of relief was enough to make Adam want to kiss Brenda. On the cheek.

'That would be lovely.' A tear ran down her cheek and Adam resisted the urge to wipe it away. Kiss her as he did so.

Rob's gaze held his for just one second too long. Long enough to tell Adam that he knew full well what the score was and that for the sake of appearances he had to leave

now. 'Good. In that case we'll make ourselves scarce while
Brenda sorts you out.' He grinned at Adam. 'Come on.
I'll buy you a cup of coffee.'

Jenna relaxed back into the sofa cushions. It was so
good to be home, not being rattled around on a trolley
or bumped along in Brenda's car. Home. Safe. There was
one more thing she wanted and he was hovering in the
doorway to the sitting room.

'Would you like some tea? Or something to eat?'

She shook her head. 'No, thanks. Why don't you come
and sit down?'

He grinned. 'Okay. Whatever you want.'

What she really wanted was a good long soak in a hot
bath. It wasn't a good idea as the heat would only make
her ankle swell even more, and she was meant to be trying to bring the swelling down. And it was definitely out
of the question with Adam there. He might have seen—
kissed—every part of her body already, but she didn't
want him to see the bruises. 'I think I just want to sit here
for a while.'

He walked over and sat down next to her. 'You'll be
stiff tomorrow.'

'I'm stiff already. It doesn't matter, it's nothing.'

He hesitated. 'I can help with that.'

Jenna chuckled. 'Yes, I know, but I'm not sure that I'm
up to that right now.' Worse luck.

His whole body tensed. 'I meant… Sorry, I wasn't…'

'It's okay.' She laid her hand on his and he almost
flinched. 'I know you didn't. So what did you mean?'

'I learned from a village midwife that you don't always
need drugs for pain.' He grinned. 'Although they do help.
Do you want to let me try a little therapeutic massage?'

'That sounds fantastic.'

He'd carried her into the bedroom and laid her on the bed, making sure she was comfortable. He started with the palms of her hands, working up her arms and then sitting her up, letting her rest her body against his, while he worked on her shoulders and back.

His fingers were sure and steady. He'd done this before with the intent to arouse, but now his whole purpose was to calm her screaming muscles. And Adam always seemed to get exactly the reaction he wanted from her body.

'Better now?' He had managed to massage her back and legs without removing her T-shirt and sweat pants, and now he'd covered her with a throw.

'Much. Tell the midwife thanks. She does good massage.'

He chuckled. 'Okay, well, just lie still for a little while and keep warm. It'll help you relax and heal.'

'Mmm. Think I will. You go and...do something...' The sentence trailed into drowsy relaxation.

When her eyes flickered open again, it was almost dark. Adam had switched a lamp on in the corner of the room, and he was sprawled in the armchair next to it. Jenna closed her eyes again. Everything was fine.

'I saw you.' His voice was relaxed, the smile running through it like a thread of gold. 'Hungry?'

Jenna opened her eyes again. 'I could eat a horse.'

He chuckled. 'Good. What do you fancy? An omelette?'

'Sounds wonderful. Thanks.' She caught his hand as he went to turn, pulling him back. 'Adam?'

'Yes. You okay, Jen?'

'I just want to know that you're okay. Are you?' He grinned and went to laugh the question off, and Jenna tugged at his hand. 'Really okay, Adam?'

He sat down next to her on the bed. 'Yes. I am. Rob made sure of that, didn't he? After you set him on me.'

He twitched at the bottom of his T-shirt. 'You want to check…?'

'That's not what I mean.'

His brow furrowed. 'No, I guess it's not, is it?' He took her hand between his and clasped it on his lap. 'I…I think we made it through.'

'We did. We did the best we could for those two men. And afterwards…' She felt tears prick at the corners of her eyes. That happened every time she thought about the terror of suddenly falling into a void. 'I know what you did, Adam. You risked your own life to come after me, and you never left me. I might not have made it if you hadn't moved me away from that pile of stuff that was about to come down on my head.'

She was trembling, two large tears rolling down her cheeks. 'Shh, honey. It's okay.' His hand brushed her cheek, its touch soothing. 'Anyone would have—'

'No, they wouldn't. You might not see that you had a choice, but that's because you're wired that way. If I'd been down there alone, I don't know whether I'd have made it out. You were the one who brought me out, Adam.'

The light that ignited in his eyes told Jenna how much that meant to him. 'Hey…' He wiped at her cheek with his thumb. 'Don't cry, Jen. Please.' He reached for a tissue from the box at the side of the bed and handed it to her. 'Actually, perhaps you should. You've been such a trouper so far. You might like to relax your guard a little now it's all over.'

'And it's good to cry, eh?' Jenna mustered a grin.

''Course it is. It ought to be mandatory after a day like today.' Suddenly he was awkward again. The man whose strength had carried her through reduced to hopeless incompetence in the face of a few tears.

'I don't much feel like it anymore. Maybe later. You can join me if you want.'

Adam laughed. 'Don't start without me. In the meantime, I'll go and get us something to eat.' He got to his feet, hesitating at the doorway, not seeming to want to take the risk of turning to look at her. 'Thanks, Jen. For trusting me.'

Then he was gone.

By the time Jenna made it through to the kitchen, he had laid a place for her at the table. Knife, fork, napkin and a rose from the climber that wound its way up the trellis behind the fire-escape steps.

'Smells good.' She made her way carefully over to the cooker and craned to see the contents of the pan in front of him.

'Go and sit down. Be ready in a minute.' He nudged her gently away. 'Go on. This is the crucial moment and I need to concentrate.'

'Oh. Don't I get to see it, then?'

'No. A guy has to retain some secrets.' Jenna made her way back to the kitchen table and he chuckled, never taking his eyes from the pan. 'You sound like the crocodile in *Peter Pan*.'

'The crocodile ticks. And it's not me squeaking, it's the crutches.'

'All the same, you won't be creeping up on anyone any time soon.' Adam bent and opened the oven, pulling out a pan and tumbling some chips onto the two plates he had waiting on the counter. Then he divided the omelette, sliding half onto each plate, and carried the plates to the table.

'Eat. Before it gets cold.'

She didn't need to be told. They ate in silence, Jenna

almost wolfing her food she was so hungry now. When she'd cleared her plate, he picked it up, putting it into the sink and switching the kettle on for tea.

'Jen, I've been thinking.' He was clearly considering his words carefully and she nodded him on. 'Don't say yes or no now, but think about it. I can delay going back to the States for a few weeks. Until you're feeling better.'

She stared at him. 'But you're needed there.'

'Nothing I can't postpone for a couple of weeks.'

Jenna couldn't believe that she was even considering saying no. 'I'm not sure that's such a good idea, Adam.'

'Will you think about it? You might feel different tomorrow.'

She might well feel differently tomorrow, but that wasn't going to change the way things were. They'd been through this before, and nothing was different.

'No, Adam. I think that we should stick to the plan. Please don't talk about this any more.' She was going to cry if he did.

Concern flashed in his eyes. 'No. I'm sorry. It's been a tough day for both of us.' He summoned up a grin from somewhere and got to his feet. 'Want a cup of tea?'

'Yes, thanks.' She caught his arm. 'Why don't we go and make ourselves comfortable in the sitting room and you can show me the notes that your colleague in America sent you?'

'Eh?' He sat back down again, opposite her.

'I want to know what you'll be doing there.' If she was going to lose him, it would be good to know that there was some purpose to it other than their mutual unwillingness to even try for something more than they already had. And to remind him of that purpose, too.

His eyes searched her face. Then understanding flooded

into them, and he nodded. 'I have pictures as well. You want to see?'

'Yes. That would be even better.' Knowing their faces, knowing their names. How could she keep him here a moment longer than planned if she could see their faces?

'I'll make the tea then go and get my laptop.'

CHAPTER FOURTEEN

'So the freezer is all stocked up.'

'Adam, there's enough in there to feed an army for a month. And if I need anything I can just order it on the internet and get it delivered.'

'Good. And where's that call button?'

'In the drawer. I don't need it when you're here, do I?'

'Yes, but you should get used to carrying it around. It's just for a few weeks, until you're a little steadier on your feet.'

'I'll carry it around.' Jenna pulled herself off the sofa and swung herself over to the dresser, opening the drawer and taking out the emergency call button that Adam had obtained. 'Honestly, I feel as if I'm eighty-five, wearing this thing. If I need anything I've always got my mobile.'

'Your mobile's where?'

'Over there.'

'Exactly. You're on your own in the house and you're unsteady on your feet. You could fall and be lying here as dead as a doornail for days before anyone found you.'

'No, I couldn't. Not with about a hundred people calling me every day. Anyway, if I were dead I wouldn't be able to press the button, would I?'

'Just work with me here, Jen.'

'Okay. I have my button. It's around my neck.' Jenna dropped the button down the front of her top. 'Happy now?'

He rolled his eyes. 'You have no idea.'

Somehow they were getting through this. By an almost superhuman effort they had managed to neither refer to nor to try and put off the parting that was getting closer by the hour. And now it was measured in minutes, rather than hours.

Adam was standing by the window, watching for something. Jenna knew what that something was. It was a car. The one that Rob drove, which would take him off to the airport and away from her.

He was wasting time. Precious minutes when something that might make sense of all of this might have been said. Something that would make them both feel better about this parting.

There was no point in thinking that way. If they hadn't come up with anything before now, an extra couple of minutes wasn't going to make any difference. Nothing was going to make this any better. It was just a matter of facing up to it and getting through it without making a fool of herself. 'What time's your flight?'

'Eight-thirty. There's plenty of time.'

'Are you all packed?'

'Pretty much.'

'Why don't you go and finish off now? Before Rob comes.' Perhaps it would be better for him to be downstairs when Rob arrived so she didn't have to see him wrenched away from her.

He turned and looked at her, reproach in his face, as if she had stolen his most prized possession. These last few moments alone. 'There's time.' He walked over to the sofa, bending down on his heels in front of her. 'There's something I wanted to say, Jenna.'

Jenna suddenly didn't want to hear it. She was coping with this—just—but if he managed to put all the things that she saw in his tawny eyes into words, she'd be devastated. 'Me, too. But maybe it's better left unsaid.'

He seemed to be debating the point with himself. 'You think so?'

'I think we know, don't we?'

'Yeah.' He dropped his gaze from hers and rose quickly. At that moment the doorbell sounded. A small cry that might have been exasperation and might have been anguish escaped his lips and he turned without a word to go and answer the door.

There was the sound of voices on the stairs and the commotion told Jenna that Rob had brought the children with him as well as Cassie. She wiped away her tears and summoned up a smile.

Ellie was first to appear, running into the sitting room ahead of the adults and flinging herself on the sofa next to Jenna. 'Dad says I mustn't touch you because you're hurt.' The child's eyes were on the cast on her foot.

'Oh, not so hurt I can't give you a hug. Hugs from you always make me feel better.' Jenna reached for Ellie and took her in her arms. The small body next to hers made her want to cry again and she bit her lip, hard.

'What did I say, Ellie?' Rob's voice boomed from the doorway.

'It's all right, Dad, I'm making Jenna feel better.' Ellie squeezed tight, as if she had the power to chase all of Jenna's hurts away.

'Well, just be a bit gentle, please.' Rob crossed the room and bent to brush a kiss on Jenna's cheek then reached for his phone, flipping it open and listening into the earpiece. 'Apparently you're in some distress.'

'What?' What had Adam been saying to him?

Rob shrugged and snapped his phone shut. 'I just got a recorded message from that emergency button of yours.'

'Oh.' Jenna shifted Ellie from her lap and found the button. 'Sorry. Must have set it off when I gave Ellie a hug.' She shot Adam an apologetic look. 'I suppose it'll be ringing everyone else on the list now.'

'No, that's okay. I accepted the message so it'll stop now. It only goes on to call the other numbers if I don't press three to say I've got the call and that I'm dealing with it.'

'So you'll know every time she hugs someone.' Adam's tone was jocular, but there was a trace of harshness there, too.

'Looks like it.' Rob grinned. 'Just make sure to take it off if you go on any hot dates.'

Cassie appeared in the doorway, shooting Rob a look that would have stopped a charging rhinoceros in its tracks. 'I don't think there's any danger of that.' She slipped her hand into the crook of Adam's arm and he looked down at her, the look of hurt anger slipping from his face. Jenna sent her a silent thank-you.

'Come on, now, Adam, give a pregnant woman your arm over to the sofa.' Cassie was blooming, heavily pregnant and, as always, the peacemaker who soothed ruffled feathers without even trying. 'I was wondering whether I might stay here with you, Jen, put my feet up for a while. We were going to take the children to see the planes at the airport, but it's too hot for me today.'

Jenna grinned. She was obviously part of Cassie's master plan. 'Yes, of course. It'll be nice to have some company.'

'Right, then.' Rob clapped his hands together, obviously eager to get going. 'Come along, mate, you never know what the traffic's going to be like.'

Cassie and Jenna sat side by side in the suddenly quiet house. Both had their feet propped up in front of them, and Jenna stared at the four sets of bare toes, trying not to cry.

Cassie blew her nose, loudly. 'I hate goodbyes.' She handed Jenna a handkerchief from the seemingly inexhaustible supply in her handbag.

If Cassie could cry, then Jenna could venture a few tears. It was almost a relief to allow herself to wipe her eyes and blow her nose. 'Me, too.'

'That's why I can never look.'

Cassie was a good friend. She had told Adam that she wouldn't watch him leave, waited for him to bend for a goodbye kiss and then resolutely clapped her hand over her eyes. When he'd brushed his lips across Jenna's cheek, he'd whispered to her to do the same. 'Close your eyes.' She'd felt Cassie's arm around her as the sounds of his footsteps had faded along the hallway and her front door had closed quietly behind him.

'Don't look back, eh?'

Cassie shrugged. 'You could put it that way. Or you could say that you'll look forward to the next time you see someone.'

There wasn't going to be a next time. She'd had her time with Adam and Jenna knew that he wouldn't be back. 'I prefer "don't look back".'

Jenna pressed her lips together. A cool calm settled around her heart, and she recognised the feeling. It was the same calm that had consumed her when Laura had died, when it had become clear that her parents weren't coming back, and when Joe had left. The calm that told her she *would* survive, come what may.

'Fancy a cup of tea?' Cassie dropped her feet down onto the floor.

'Stay there. I'll make it.' Jenna slid to the edge of the sofa and got to her feet. 'I'm getting a bit tired of being looked after.'

They sipped their tea and talked a little and then watched a film together, an old weepie. Cassie cried, and Jenna stared impassively at the screen. Who cared? It didn't really matter if two people met, fell in love and then had to part. There were more important things in life.

'Aren't you due soon?' Cassie had been trying to get comfortable on the sofa and had obviously failed miserably.

'Another two weeks. Ellie and Daisy were both late, so I reckon it'll probably be three.'

'Perhaps it'll be sooner. They get earlier each time.'

Cassie rolled her eyes. 'Well, I hope so. I've got…' She tailed off, clapping her hand over her mouth. 'Jenna, I'm sorry.'

'What's the matter, Cass?' Something in her friend's tone told her that there was something.

'My water's just broke.' Cassie moaned in embarrassment. 'Oh, dear, Jen, your sofa.'

Jenna was on her feet more quickly than she'd thought possible. 'Forget the sofa. Are you sure?'

'Oh, yes.' Cassie's hand went to her side and she gasped for breath. 'Jen, I'm so sorry.'

'Hey, there.' She gave Cassie a bright smile. 'Just concentrate on the baby. Stay there for a moment and I'll get you a towel.'

Jenna pulled some clean towels from the cupboard and

fetched her stethoscope from the bottom of the wardrobe. When she got back, Cassie was trying to stand.

'All right, just sit back here.' She got Cassie comfortable and reached for her stethoscope, which had fallen onto the floor. 'Contractions?'

'Yes.' Cassie caught her breath again. 'I thought it was just backache at first. Then I thought it was a Higgs-Boson.'

'Braxton-Hicks. How long for?'

'Couple of hours. Maybe longer. They're getting stronger, Jen.' Cassie's eyes were wide with panic.

'Okay, okay. No problem. I've delivered babies before and even if it comes now, everything's going to be all right. Just relax.' Now was not the time for the truth. Jenna had seen a baby being delivered. She knew what was supposed to happen. She propped a cushion behind Cassie's head and started to pray.

'Thank goodness.' Cassie's hand found hers and gripped tight. 'Rob hasn't, you know.'

'Well, just as well this happened when you were with me. Now, do you have your prenatal stuff?'

'In my handbag. Listen, don't go pressing that emergency button of yours, Rob's going to have kittens. And he's got the kids with him in the car.'

'It's okay. This is not an emergency, you're having a baby. We've both done this before.' Jenna grinned encouragingly and Cassie smiled back. 'Good. Just hold on there and let me call the hospital.' Jenna found the number in Cassie's handbag and hobbled over to the phone.

CHAPTER FIFTEEN

JENNA held the baby in her arms, Rob's arm steadying her at the side of the font. One month old. She made her promises, solemnly and carefully. To keep James from harm. To care for him if there was ever a time when his parents couldn't. She knew just how much of a responsibility that was, and she took it seriously. James would always have a home with her, any time he needed it.

Ignoring the tall figure standing on the other side of the font, she concentrated on the words of the christening ceremony. Rob took the baby from her and he began to whimper fretfully.

'They say it's good luck if the baby cries.' Adam caught up with her as she planted her crutches on the stone steps leading out of the church. 'Want a hand?' He held out his arm towards her.

Jenna ignored it and made it down the steps on her own. 'So you made it back? Rob and Cassie didn't think you would.' Outside in the sunlight he looked almost dazzling. He wore a lightweight off-white suit with a crisp white shirt, open at the neck, which contrasted with his tan. His long, sun-bleached hair was slicked back, making him look even more striking. The last month had obviously been kind to him. Kinder than it had to her.

'Only just. I'm straight off the plane. My bags are in Rob's car. I hear you delivered our new godchild.'

Our child. The two words suddenly leapt out of the sentence and collided with each other. Jenna swallowed hard. 'Well, I did the sitting-down bits. The paramedic arrived just in time and did the running around. Cassie did all the work.'

'I heard you did a fantastic job.' His eyes searched her face and Jenna tried hard not to flinch under the scrutiny. 'I pulled out all the stops to get here, Jen. This is important.'

'Yes.' She tore herself away from his gaze. 'I've just seen my lift. I'll see you back at the house.' Jenna hobbled away from him, aware that he was following her retreat with his eyes, but she was determined not to turn around.

Jenna had offered her garden for the christening party, and Rob and Cassie had accepted, descending on her with an army of helpers who insisted that she didn't lift a finger. Which was just as well, because it was taking all her time and energy to avoid Adam.

He almost caught her in the garden by the drinks table, but she gave him the slip and found Cassie in her bedroom, feeding the baby. Pleading tiredness, she stayed upstairs while Cassie went back down so that James could be passed around the guests one final time.

Okay, so it was rude. But Cassie would smooth things over, she always did. And Jenna couldn't bear to go downstairs, say hello to Adam, hear about all the great things he'd been doing in the last month, and then watch him go again. Finally, the sound of crockery being washed and stacked in the empty downstairs flat subsided, and Cassie walked into Jenna's bedroom, not bothering to knock, and sat down on the bed.

'You can come out now.'

Was she that transparent? 'Sorry, Cass. I just didn't want...'

'I know. It's okay, everyone understood. You were tired and needed to lie down.' Cassie grinned at her.

'You're a star, you know that?'

'I do my best. And you're the one who's the star, letting us have the run of your place for the party. I don't think everyone would have fitted in our garden.'

'It's a pleasure. Glad to help, you know that.'

'Thanks.' Cassie leaned forward and kissed her cheek. 'Well, Rob's stacking the kids away in the car, so we'll be off. Anything we can do for you before we go?'

'No, I'm fine. Go home and put your feet up.' The silence in the house pressed down on her like a heavy load. A heavy load that wasn't going to be lifted any time soon.

'Still missing him?' Cassie didn't move.

'No. Well, maybe a bit.'

'You should talk to him.'

Jenna shrugged. 'There isn't much point, is there? Look at him, Cass. He looks...' He looked like a new man. Adam still, but without the cares that had dogged him so stubbornly. 'He'll be going back soon.'

'Okay.' Cassie gave up surprisingly easily. Maybe she was tired, too. It had been a long day. 'Rob'll be round tomorrow to pick you up for lunch.'

That silence again. Cassie's footsteps had echoed down the stairs and Jenna had heard the front door close. She took a deep breath. Don't mope. Get up, put your happy face on, even though there's no one here to see it.

She drew back the curtains and smoothed her hands over her dress, looking at herself in the mirror. She liked this dress. White, flowing, with pale embroidery all over the bodice. The thought that she was glad that she'd been wearing something nice when Adam saw her filtered through her defences, and she slammed it back.

Suddenly she couldn't bear to wear the dress anymore. She slipped out of it, almost tearing it as she hopped on one foot and rolled backwards onto the bed. Slipping into the sweat pants that she'd already decided to burn the minute she got rid of this cast, a T-shirt and a cardigan, she made her way out onto the balcony.

Looking down, she saw a figure sitting on the fire-escape steps, his long tawny hair bright in the evening sun. His elbows were resting on his knees, and he was obviously waiting for someone. And that someone could only be her.

'Adam.' She couldn't bring herself to say anything else. She wanted to turn, go back into the house, slam the balcony door closed and wait till he went away. But she couldn't.

He looked up, his direct gaze just as unsettling as it had ever been. When he caught sight of her, he smiled. 'Jen.'

'What are you doing here? I thought that Cass and Rob had left.'

'They have. I didn't go with them.' He stood up, his eyes never leaving her. 'I came here to talk to you.'

She shook her head. 'You came for James's christening.' She didn't want to hear any lies from him. He'd never lied to her before and now was no time to start.

'I was coming anyway. For you.'

Jenna's knees wobbled and she hung on to her crutches. 'Don't say that, Adam.'

He shrugged. 'Okay. But it's the truth.' He was still looking up at her. 'Can I talk to you, Jen? Please.'

'I'll come down.' Jenna grasped the handrail of the balcony firmly, hanging on tight while she walked down the steps. Even her good leg felt as if it couldn't bear her weight.

He ran up the steps towards her. 'Let me help you.'

'I'm okay, thanks.' The thought of his touch was the last straw, and she swayed dangerously, before strong hands fastened themselves around her waist.

'Here, you'll fall. Don't make me have to patch you up again.' He kept tight hold of her arm, guiding her down until she was on the patio. Jenna sank down onto the steps.

'Thank you. Thank you for coming down. For hearing what I've got to say.'

She forced a smile. 'I haven't heard it yet. Anyway, if I hadn't, you'd have still been there tomorrow morning, wouldn't you?' She knew him well enough for that.

'And the day after. May I sit with you?'

Those silly little things that he had used to do so naturally, and that he was asking her permission to do now. Touching her, sitting next to her. It was as if everything that they had once had was now lost. Something twisted, deep down in her stomach. This was worse than losing him the first time.

'Of course.'

He sat next to her, one arm on the step behind her, his body not touching hers. 'Jen, I won't take much of your time. Just a few minutes, and then I'll go.'

'That's fine, Adam. Take as much time as you want.' Yet another lie. Since when had so many lies stood between them?

He took a moment, as if he were flipping through a set of mental notes, reminding himself where he wanted to begin. 'It ripped my heart out to leave you, Jen. I did it because I thought it was the right thing to do. I couldn't see past my own fears and I knew that I couldn't give you what you needed.' Jenna opened her mouth to speak, but he held up his hand. 'Hear me out. Please.'

The anguish in his voice stopped her short. 'Okay. Go on.'

'When I went back to Florida, I did everything I could to try and remember, hanging on to the hope that I might still be someone who could care for you. I went to a hypnotherapist, pulled the medical and crime reports from that day and studied every word of them.'

'And you know now what happened?' He must do. There was nothing else that could explain the way he stood taller now, as if a heavy load had been lifted from his shoulders.

'No. I realised that even though I want to know what happened, it wouldn't change anything. I'd still be second-guessing myself, indulging in what-ifs. But time and time again I kept coming back to one thing. That I trust and respect you. And that if you could find it in your heart to trust me, the way you did in that basement, I'd better start living up to that.'

Trust. Respect. Two very fine words. Jenna swallowed down her disappointment. 'That's good, Adam. It's great.'

He seemed to sense her lack of enthusiasm. 'What I'm trying to say to you, Jen, is that I can change. I have changed. Not by delving around in the past, looking for things that might not be there. But by loving you. Being loved by you, and wanting to be the man who deserves that love.'

'No.' The word whispered in her throat. She could hardly comprehend, let alone believe, what he was saying to her.

'Yes, Jen.' He took hold of her hand and hung on to it possessively. 'I know that I abandoned you. And after everything that's happened, that was the worst thing I could have done to you. But I do love you. I can't offer you my past, but everything that I am now, everything I will be is yours. And I might not have any right to ask this, but I want you to forgive me.'

She pulled her hand away from his. 'No.' Jenna could feel the tears rising in her throat. 'No, you can't mean that.' She didn't know what to do with this sudden confession of his. Didn't know how to respond, when no one else had said anything like that to her before.

'I mean it.' He reached into the open neck of his shirt and pulled out a chain, which had something dangling from it. 'I know that you probably can't trust me now, but I want to show you something.'

Jenna focussed through her tears. It was a ring. Sparkling in the evening sunlight.

'This is yours, Jen, whenever you want to take it. Until then, I'll keep it safe for you as a sign of my intentions.'

She reached out and touched it. It was beautiful. Its fire seemed to burn her fingers, and she snatched them away. 'I...I don't know what to say, Adam. This is...unexpected.'

'I know. I'm not asking for your answer now.' His lips twisted in regret. 'In fact, I don't want to hear your answer yet. I'll warn you in advance that I'm aiming for a *yes* and nothing much else is going to do.'

She grinned at him. It was one of the things she loved about Adam. So charming, but underneath it all he was as solid as a rock. 'What's that engraved on the inside?' He'd gone to put the ring away, sliding it back inside his shirt, but she wanted to look at it a while longer. Fix it in her mind, so she could believe.

His face lit up. He knew they'd taken that first step. He held the ring steady so she could see properly. 'It says *"True North"*. You see the diamond?'

It was hardly possible to miss it. It wasn't exactly small. 'Yes.' Jenna stared at the ring.

'Well, I looked at hundreds of rings, trying to decide which one was good enough. Then I saw this one, and it reminded me of something, back at the observatory. The Pole Star. The one star that's guided men for centuries, helped them find their way. You're my true north, Jen, my only direction from now on.'

A tear rolled down her cheek. 'You'll always find your way back, wherever you are.' He'd come a long way in the last month. But maybe he hadn't travelled quite as far as she had hoped.

'No.' He shook his head. 'I never want to leave you.'

'But your work?' That was always going to come between them. Always going to take him away.

'That's important to me. But there are lots of ways that I can do what I do, and travelling's just one of them. I can stay in Florida, or here, and specialise in major cases.' He hesitated and took a breath. 'Or, if you want to, you can travel with me.'

She could see how hard that was for him to say. But it was the only thing left that she still wanted from him. 'You mean...go with you...to South America?'

'Wherever the work takes us, if that's what you want. I can't tell you that I'll never be concerned for your safety, or that I won't do everything I can to protect you, but I won't clip your wings.' He raised a trembling hand to her cheek, brushing away her tears.

'It's easy to say, Adam.' She couldn't believe he meant it. Didn't dare.

'I know. That's what I mean about true north. Any time I need reminding of the right course to take, I'll know where to go.' His lips curved in a smile. 'To someone who's more than capable of telling me I'm an idiot and giving me a good shake.'

She nudged his shoulder with hers. 'You're an idiot.'

'See?' He raised trembling fingers to her cheek, tilting her face towards his. 'I won't let you down, Jen.'

'I know. I need… This is all so sudden, Adam. I need to slow down.'

'Take your time, honey, I'll wait.'

It was his final, precious gift. He knew that she needed a little time, and he wasn't going to push her until she'd come around to the idea that there was someone in this world who would never leave her. That *he* would never leave her.

'Want to come inside? You can wait there, if you like.'

They were in Cornwall. Just for a few days, before Jenna was due to go back to the hospital to have X-rays and to get rid of the cast on her leg. The last week had been magical. Adam had never left her side. He had repeated his promises to her, as many times as she had wanted to hear them, and slowly the wounds that she had hidden for so long had begun to heal.

'Would you like to go down to the beach? There's a full moon tonight.' Their hotel was just a short walk from the sheltered, sandy cove that was almost deserted after the sun went down.

'Yes. I'd like that.' Maybe that would be the place.

He strolled with her along the gently sloping cliff path, and carried her down the steps and to the water's edge. The moon was large and low, tipping the dark waves with silver.

She hung on to his waist, not for support but just because she wanted him close. His arm around her shoulders, keeping her warm in the night breeze. This was the place.

'When you get that cast off your leg, and it's a bit stronger, I'll teach you how to surf, if you like.' His eyes were on the sea.

'I'd like that. Might come in handy, living in Florida.' The words sounded so right. So full of promise.

'What did you say?' He turned slowly, as if unable to believe his ears.

'That I'd have a go at surfing.'

'No, you didn't. You said it would come in handy, living in Florida.'

'Did I?' Jenna assumed a look of exaggerated innocence.

'I heard you quite plainly. Florida, you said. Living in Florida.'

'Hmm. Suppose I must have done, then.'

He twisted round, falling to one knee in front of her, holding on to her waist to steady her. 'Here.' He pulled her down onto his knee. 'I don't want you falling over, right in the middle of this.'

He had a point. Her legs were already shaking. Her fingers too as she reached around his neck and unclasped the chain, putting the ring into his palm. She'd seen it many times now, but it was still as beautiful as when she'd first laid eyes on it.

'Jenna, this isn't a request, I'm going to insist on it. You *are* going to marry me.'

She could feel his heartbeat. So strong. So true. And right now it was racing, as if it couldn't wait for everything the future held.

'Yes, Adam. I am going to marry you.'

He slipped the ring on to her finger and it looked just

as she had imagined it would there. 'Where's the North Star?' She tilted her head towards the night sky.

'Right here, honey.' He kissed her, and suddenly the course ahead was clear. 'True North.'

* * * * *

A sneaky peek at next month...

Medical Romance™

CAPTIVATING MEDICAL DRAMA—WITH HEART

My wish list for next month's titles...

In stores from 4th May 2012:

❏ Sydney Harbour Hospital: Lexi's Secret – Melanie Milburne

& West Wing to Maternity Wing! – Scarlet Wilson

❏ Diamond Ring for the Ice Queen – Lucy Clark

& No.1 Dad in Texas – Dianne Drake

❏ The Dangers of Dating Your Boss – Sue MacKay

& The Doctor, His Daughter and Me – Leonie Knight

Available at WHSmith, Tesco, Asda, Eason, Amazon and Apple

Just can't wait?